Dragged, terrified, from
by an arrogant Roman
journey to Imperial Rom
is determined to escape.
is really Thelia, long-lost daug...
But how can this be when she has been brought up to
dislike and distrust all Romans?

Who can she trust in decadent Rome? Not Octavia her
beautiful 'sister', nor her compatriot the gladiator Gregor. Only her determination to tell the proud Flavius
exactly what she thinks of his ruthless treatment spurs
her on to learn his language and plot her revenge.

To Aunty Ciss & Uncle Horace with love from Elaine x

By the same author in Masquerade

LADY IN THE LION'S DEN

My Daughter Thelia

Elaine Reeve

MILLS & BOON LIMITED
London · Sydney · Toronto

*First published in Great Britain 1983
by Mills & Boon Limited, 15–16 Brook's Mews,
London W1A 1DR*

© Elaine Reeve 1983
*Australian copyright 1983
Philippine copyright 1983*

ISBN 0 263 74486 8

The text of this publication or any part thereof may not be reproduced or transmitted in any form or by any means, electronic or mechanical, including photocopying, recording, storage in an information retrieval system, or otherwise, without the written permission of the publisher.

This book is sold subject to the condition that it shall not, by way of trade or otherwise, be lent, resold, hired out or otherwise circulated without the prior consent of the publisher in any form of binding or cover other than that in which it is published and without a similar condition including this condition being imposed on the subsequent purchaser.

Set in 10 on 12 pt Linotron Times
04/1283

*Photoset by Rowland Phototypesetting Ltd
Bury St Edmunds, Suffolk
Made and printed in Great Britain by
Cox & Wyman Ltd, Reading*

CHAPTER ONE

SHE cowered down into the bush, willing herself to shrink, and biting her lips against involuntary whimpers of pain as the vicious thorns scratched and gouged at every part of her flesh. Fear kept her rigid and silent, her breath held and every muscle and nerve tense; her ragged nails dug painfully into the palm of her hand.

It seemed an eternity that she crouched there, the long line of Roman soldiers, helmets glinting in the afternoon sun, marching along the moorland track, pressing north. Ever northwards. Would there be no stopping them now? There had been such hope, such courage and excitement when Boudicca had raised a great army to bring them down. How fierce and splendid she had looked; how formidable the people. But all for nothing, in the end, for they had plunged on to their ultimate destruction, driven by obsession and drunk with success. It was easy, now, to say that it had been inevitable. The Romans were well ensconced in their forts and their villas; protected by their garrisons and their formidable soldiers and thrusting ever northwards with their roads. Folly to have tried to stop them so late . . .

Eventually, the last of the soldiers on that track marched past. But she waited until she was certain she was safe and then rose stiffly and rubbed at her aching, bloody legs. She was thin; too thin. But she was a striking creature with dark-blue eyes, large in her small pointed face, and hair that was long and thick and a deep dark red. A strange colour, that set her apart from others.

She had been found as a small child, near-starving and half frozen, by a group of the Iceni, who had taken her in as one of their own. For many days she had spoken only one word, a word that sounded like 'thea', and that had become her name, whether or not it was a name. It was after the failure of the great rebellion and Boudicca's death by her own hand, that many of the Iceni, and Thea with them, had fled north in small groups to endure the privations of a harsh winter. And now, these past few days, the Romans had appeared here, even in this remote part where they had thought themselves free.

She replaced the knife she had been gripping so tightly in the belt of her tunic and looked down at the dead fawn at her feet. It made her feel ill to think that she had killed it, but its mother had been savaged and half-eaten by wolves and the fawn was near dead with starvation and fear anyway. She did not like to hunt—except to fish, which was different—it was men's work and she had no stomach for it. But it had been kinder to kill the poor creature swiftly than to leave it to die slowly, and it would help the scant food supplies. Her own meagre catch—a mere dozen undersized fish from the ice-cold lake—would scarce feed even the babes. She enjoyed fishing; quite happily, now that the weather was turned warmer, she would sit on the edge of the lake, gazing at the seemingly depthless waters, glad to escape the squabbling of the other women and the petulant demands of the children.

She sighed and bent down to drag the fawn up over her shoulder. Grasping her string of fish in her other hand, she set off across the rough ground to the track along which the Romans had gone.

She narrowed her eyes against the sun and looked down the track after them, but they were out of sight beyond the hill. Shifting her burden slightly, she turned her back and began the long walk home. 'Home' was a pitiful collection of rough buildings huddled together in the lee of a rugged escarpment; but it was, for now at least, as safe and welcoming a place as any.

The sun was low in the sky when she arrived and the few store huts and work buildings were deserted. By now everyone would have gathered in the long, low building in which, whatever their various pursuits and diversions of the day, they all came together as the sun set and dusk closed in.

Thea, her shoulder aching from her burden, made her way towards it and went inside. She eased the dead fawn onto a long table and dropped her bundle of fish beside it. She looked across at the girl who stood on the other side. 'Wolves killed its mother and it was half-dead anyway,' she explained and added, 'there are Romans up on the moor, Brede.'

'Romans?' the girl repeated anxiously. 'Many? Did they see you?'

Thea shrugged. 'Half a cohort, perhaps less. And marching north. They did not see me, though I doubt it would have mattered. They are not interested in us. We are not a threat now.'

'But you must be careful. You are a woman after all and the Romans are animals. Why must you go out to fish every day, and alone? 'Tis not as if—'

'We have few enough men to hunt,' she interrupted. 'It is good that I can help, for we need all the food we can get and while that sort of hunting,' she indicated the fawn, 'sickens me, I enjoy fishing.' She smiled, a little wryly. 'The fish did not bite so well today, though.'

She did not add that to spend her days tending the children, cooking, stitching pelts and skins, patching tunics, curing leather for shields and belts and collecting wood for fires and spears, would be more than she could bear. It was not that she objected to these tasks—she did what she had to with good grace. But she relished the independence that fishing gave her, and the freedom from the confines of the makeshift settlement and the petty squabbles that permeated the days. She enjoyed the tranquillity of the lake and she enjoyed her isolation. And sometimes she did feel very isolated. Brede was her only true friend—more like a sister—since it was Brede's family who had taken her in. She felt close to no-one else.

She knew she was different. She was not of the Iceni and although she had grown up among them and knew no other way of life, still there was something that kept her a little aloof, and it was not merely that she was from some other tribe. It was something that caused the young men to pass comments and make suggestive remarks to her but never to touch her or attempt to waylay her and snatch a kiss. They kept their distance and treated her differently. Yet they liked her and admired her because she was pretty and could fish as well as they, and run as fast—or faster. But there was something else that made them wary. She was just different. Only very occasionally did she allow herself to substitute 'better' for 'different'.

They ate quite well that night. The winter had been hard and hungry and it was so good now to feel the warmth of the sun by day and the reassurance of a full belly at night. How nice it would be, Thea thought, if I only knew I would never again be hungry. But she was well aware that come next winter, it would take a miracle to keep away those gnawing pains in her stomach; she could only, now, give thanks for the bounties of spring and summer, and savour the wonderful feeling of fullness that gave her, if only briefly, a sense of well-being and comfort.

The following day, she went out with her line again and pushed the little coracle that was kept moored in the weeds out into the lake and there spent several hours in blessed solitude. It was a warm day with the gentlest of breezes and, by the time the sun was high, she had doubled the previous day's haul. So she drew the boat to the shore, tied it up safely and clambered out to collapse gladly on the rough heather and lie there on her stomach, at the very edge, looking down into the surface of the water, where it was dark and still and smooth amongst the reeds. She twisted up the cloud of her hair and piled it on top of her head, arranging it this way and that and studying her reflection in the water. It was infuriating that the image was always slightly blurred and swayed gently so that she could not see clearly, but she thought perhaps she was prettier than Brcde, than any of them. Or could be, if only—A sudden angry frustration welled up in her and she brought her hand down sharply, slapping the water and dissolving the face in a dozen erratic ripples.

She turned onto her back and let the sun warm her again, watching the birds that glided across the blue sky, thinking how it must be to be one of them, and growing drowsy.

The dull thundering of hoofs gradually penetrated her daydreams. With a startled gasp, she sat bolt upright, wide-eyed and suddenly fearful. Too late she realised the folly of moving for she had been seen, and they were Romans! Some eight or nine of them out for sport, for she could see the game slung across the horses as they rode towards her. There was no hiding from them this time.

She scrambled to her feet, instinctively pulling the knife from her belt, and half-fell, half-crawled towards the rope securing the boat. She managed to undo the loose knot but in her haste dropped the knife, and as she made a desperate lunge after it to rescue it from the weeds on which it lay, the rope slipped from her trembling fingers. The knife sank into the water and she could only watch in despair as the little boat drifted quickly out of reach. She thought, for a moment, of plunging in after it, but the icy depths were daunting and she was caught between two dangers equally terrifying.

Her hesitation cost her the opportunity of regaining the boat in any event; the Romans were almost upon her and as they drew up their horses and dismounted, she turned and ran, praying to any god that might hear that they were too well fed and too used to riding to be able to run fast.

Behind her, she heard what must have been a curse, then laughter and shouts and in another moment, light and fast though she was, the breath was knocked from her thin body as she was hurled to the ground with the full weight of a man on top of her.

Her face was pressed into the coarse, fragrant heather; she felt warm breath on her neck and a voice murmuring what she was sure were obscenities in her ear. But suddenly she was free of him as he was dragged from her amid coarse laughter and she was hauled abruptly to her feet. To her dismay, she was surrounded by them. Her heart thudded painfully with fear as she spun round and stared at the leering, laughing faces. Abruptly she threw herself at the gap between two of them only to be caught in unyielding arms and pushed back. Others caught her, and as she twisted desperately away she was forced to her knees.

A face came close to hers; a hand gripped the back of her neck, fingers entwined in her long hair and pulled her head back. As she cried out, a mouth came down on hers to stifle the sound and kiss her. Somehow, she managed to twist her face away and lash out at the man before her, which had only the effect of causing the rest of them to roar with laughter and goad him on. His hands were moving all over her body, and, sick with fear and loathing, she struggled furiously and felt, rather than heard, the stitching at the neck of her tunic tear apart.

Then, suddenly, across the noisy enjoyment of her captors, there came another voice. Deep and quiet, it yet had an authority about it and although it spoke only a word, the men around Thea were stilled and after a moment fell away and left her in a crumpled, dishevelled heap on the ground. Relief brought the sting of tears to her eyes. She bowed her head and clutched the tunic across her chest, and with her other hand brushed her long tangled hair from her face.

The silence was broken only by her own gasping breath and the gentle lapping of the lake water against the bank. She swallowed hard and raised her eyes to look at the man who owned the voice. He sat astride a big horse and was looking down at her strangely. He spoke to her, not unkindly and obviously a question, but beyond that she did not understand him and could only look at him blankly. He continued to stare at her and she returned his gaze steadily, despite her fear. It would be useless to try to run. She had no choice but to wait and see what he did. Oh, how she regretted her blessed solitude now!

Something in his face had changed. There was an intentness in his expression, a narrowing of his eyes. He spoke sharply to her, but she could only shrug her shoulders and shake her head. He turned his head slightly then and asked something of the men around him, but received only shakes of heads and murmured dissent in reply. He beckoned her closer and continued to stare intently at her as she got to her feet and moved reluctantly forward. With a suddenness that made her start, he lifted one leg over his horse and sprang to the ground.

He reached out, grasped her arm and pulled her closer. As he did so she lost her grip on the top of her tunic and with a sharp intake of breath, his other hand reached up to touch her. She drew swiftly back, but he tightened his grip and said something softly which she took to be reassurance, then he touched the medallion which was hanging, as it had always done, around her neck. His interest in it disturbed her, but when she tried to pull away, he merely increased the pressure of his hand on her arm. He released the medallion and, grasping her chin roughly, he forced her head up.

He was obviously startled. His whole manner now was one of intent interest and Thea saw something that might almost be recognition in his eyes. Suppose—she began to shake at the thoughts that were racing through her head—suppose the medallion had been stolen, all those years ago? Suppose—Abruptly she struggled to be free of him. 'What do you want with me?' she cried. 'Why do you stare at me? Let me go. Please, let me go!'

He did not understand her, of course. He shook her

hard and she gave up her struggles and stood limply, aware of his superior strength. He pointed a finger at his chest. 'Fla-vi-us,' he said distinctly, and repeated, 'Flavius.'

Suspiciously, she nodded, understanding well enough that it was what he was called. Then he pointed at her, and raised his eyebrows expectantly. 'Thea,' she said quietly, and then lifted her head and said more strongly: 'My name is Thea. I am of the Iceni. You must release me and let me return to—'

He cut across her words abruptly and turning to his companions spoke quickly, touching her hair and her medallion, pointing to her eyes and mentioning her name several times. Did he indeed recognise something about her? Did he think she had stolen the charm? Had he taken a liking to her looks and wanted her for himself? Perhaps he was thinking she would fetch a good slave price? Bewildered, fearing that something terrible was about to happen to her, she could only stand squirming helplessly in his grasp and wait.

The ensuing discussion was somewhat heated but Flavius evidently had superiority of rank and after a very few minutes waved aside all opposition, said something in a chilling tone and proceeded to pull Thea towards his horse. 'You cannot do this!' she screamed, struggling frantically, 'I will not go with you! I will not!'

But she did go with him, if only because she was not given any other choice. She was picked up bodily and deposited on his horse and, without waiting for his companions to collect their own scattered animals, he rode off with her, skirting the end of the lake and striking out across the sun-warmed loneliness of the moor.

There was little discussion between the men as they rode across the moor. Thea stared into the distance, searching for some sign of a destination. With every lenghtening stride of the horses' hoofs her fear increased and her hopes of ever being able to find her way safely back to the escarpment diminished. There was little to be gained by trying to throw herself off his horse, she could not out-run them and it was more than likely she would stumble as she jumped and be crushed beneath the hoofs of the horses behind.

They reached a track eventually and turned along it. It was a wide, straight and level road cut by Romans into the roughness of the uneven moor; not embedded with flat, smooth stones as those she had seen built in the south, but still unmistakably Roman. It seemed only to go to a fort that Thea had not even realised existed, but then they were, by now, a long way from the settlement and she had never before strayed further across the lonely wilderness than the lake.

Flavius pulled her roughly from the horse and drew her towards the collection of buildings; but suddenly she kicked hard at his ankles, wrenched free of him and ran back to the horses. It was a useless thing to have attempted and it gained her nothing but an undignified entry into the fort—for he caught her, slung her across his shoulder and carried her inside the nearest building. Treated like a carcass! She pounded his back with her fists and kicked her knees into his chest, calling him every vile name she knew, all without the slightest effect, until she was suddenly set down on a pile of dirty sacks in what was obviously some kind of storeroom.

He stood looking at her. It was gloomy, for the door admitted little light, but she could see that he was amused. She could also see, now that she really looked at him, that he was tall and deceptively lean—she had already felt the muscular power of his arms and did not doubt the strength of the rest of his body. His dark, almost black hair curled in the nape of his neck and onto his forehead above dark brown eyes; his jaw was square and sharply defined, and his whole bearing was proud, taut and self-assured. He said something, but she could draw no encouragement from the tone of his voice and merely glared at him. He turned away and left her there, closing and barring the door, plunging her into a darkness so thick she thought she would suffocate in it. She sat quite still, staring into the blackness, afraid to move and trembling with anger and frustration, one hand fingering the medallion and the other clenched into a fist.

She did not have to wait long. He returned with two men, took her firmly by the arm and pulled her to her feet. She went meekly enough; there seemed little point in trying to break free of him for the two soldiers followed closely behind and she had no chance of escaping. She was taken along a narrow passage, out into the open and into a small building which stood alone in the corner of a courtyard. They passed soldiers who glanced with curiosity at Thea and either saluted Flavius silently or made laughing comments to him. Thea longed to spit in their ugly Roman faces, but she clenched her teeth and was silent.

Flavius did not salute the man who awaited them, but merely nodded. He pushed Thea down onto a fur-covered bench standing against the wall and made some comments about her to the centurion, who turned to look at her in the same intent way. He came across to her, the metal on his uniform tunic clinking as he walked. He, too, held her medallion and examined it and she struck his hand away angrily. 'I did not take it!' she cried. 'It was mine when they found me.'

The centurion ignored her and spoke to Flavius, who shrugged, spoke quietly and gestured towards her several times. She sat growing increasingly agitated and glared back when the Centurion looked her up and down and continued to look at her whilst talking to Flavius. Then he came closer again and bent down so that his face was level with hers, and began to ask questions. He evidently thought that by speaking slowly and clearly and far too loudly she would suddenly be endowed with the power to understand him.

Angry, frightened and confused, Thea suddenly sprang to her feet, knocking the centurion over and causing Flavius to chuckle, which only served to add to her fury. 'Why do you do this to me?' she cried, her eyes blazing and her whole body trembling. 'Why do you ask me questions you know I cannot answer because I don't understand? What do you want of me? Why have you brought me here? I do not understand what I have done!' Her voice ended, to her shame, in a petulant wail and tears, unbidden, sprang into her eyes and spilled and she turned away and sank on to the seat, weeping silently.

Despite her despair, Thea heard the two men conferring quietly and one of them left the room. She drew a shuddering breath, summoning courage, and slowly raised her head. Flavius was standing with folded arms, watching her, unsmiling and expressionless, quite still but looking almost predatory. He reminded her of an eagle: his nose was like the eagle's beak, his hands had the power of talons and his eyes sometimes had the mesmerising quality of an eagle's unblinking stare. She shivered, and turned her face away, drawing her knees into the circle of her arms and resting her chin upon them for comfort.

MY DAUGHTER THELIA 17

When the centurion returned, he had with him a shabbily dressed young man. Thea looked at him with wary curiosity, suspicious and sullen, and turned away again as the three of them stood discussing her in low voices.

'Your name is "Thea"?' The newcomer stood over her and pronounced her name uncertainly. 'I am Agrippa.'

She looked up at him in a flood of relief. 'You speak my language!' She glanced across at Flavius and smiled wryly. 'At last they have had the sense to bring someone who understands me! What do they think I have done?'

'I do not think they suspect you of anything,' he said, and sat down beside her. 'You say your name is Thea?' She nodded. 'What age are you?'

She shrugged. 'I do not know. Why?'

'You must have some idea how old you are.'

But Thea was suspicious. 'Why? Why do you—they—want to know? What do they want with me?'

'If you want to help yourself,' he said, 'I think you should answer all their questions. They mean you no harm.'

Thea did not at all want to answer any questions, but she could see that she had no other choice if she wanted to go home before nightfall. 'I have been with the Iceni fifteen years,' she said grudgingly, 'and they say I was no more than two years old when they found me, perhaps less.'

'So you are sixteen? Seventeen?' Thea shrugged and nodded. 'You say you were found. Where?'

'In the south somewhere. Where the Canti live, I think. I do not know the exact place.'

'The charm round your neck. Did the Iceni give it to you?'

'No,' she said warily, 'it is mine. I have always had it. I had it when they found me.' She paused, then put a tentative hand on his arm. 'Please make them tell me what they want. They cannot keep me here like this and tell me nothing.'

He nodded and spoke at some length to Flavius, who replied slowly, seeming reluctant but eventually shrugging and nodding.

'They think, or at least Flavius does,' Agrippa told her, 'that you are the daughter of Pontius Aquila, one of Rome's richest and most powerful men, who spent several years in the south of Britain as a garrison commander, with his wife and family. His two youngest children were twins, Marcus and Thelia, and when they were no more than babes, there was an uprising of the Canti and the twins disappeared. Marcus was found unharmed a few days later but they never found Thelia and Pontius and his family eventually returned to Rome. Flavius is a friend of the family and he says you look very like Marcus. The unusual colour of your hair and eyes are too alike to be coincidence and most convincing of all is the medallion. Apparently Marcus has one identical and so does Octavia, Pontius's eldest daughter. The centurion confirms that the emblem on the medallion is that of Pontius's family although he does not personally know them.'

Thea said nothing, struggling to digest the story. Daughter of a Roman? She felt a little sick. She hated Romans. She could not possibly be a Roman's daughter. Slowly she shook her head. 'It cannot be true. Perhaps the charm was given to me by someone who found it. Perhaps—' she added desperately, 'my real parents stole it for me.'

Flavius put in a word, obviously asking what she had

MY DAUGHTER THELIA

said, and there was a brief exchange between him and Agrippa, who then said to Thea: 'He says it is nonsense. There are too many coincidences for there to be any doubt—he is convinced.'

Thea remained silent, bewildered and appalled. The centurion spoke in his quiet voice and Agrippa said: 'Are you hungry? Tired? I can take you somewhere where you can rest and eat while they decide what is to be done.'

Too stunned and confused to do anything else, she nodded. It was not until he was leading her across the courtyard that his last words sank in. 'What do they have to decide? About me? What will they do?' Agrippa did not answer. She had seen what Romans could do and she did not underestimate them. 'I am not who he thinks I am,' she insisted quietly, more to herself than to him, fearful of the unknown fate she seemed suddenly to be in danger of having thrust upon her.

Agrippa offered neither answers nor reassurance, only a sympathetic half-smile as he drew her into a small, sparsely furnished room and there left her, with a promise to bring her some food, which she knew she would not be able to eat, and a guard outside the door to prevent her leaving.

She sat and stared into nothingness. A Roman's daughter? She was horrified, and yet at the same time, deep in her heart, she was prepared to believe it. The words which Agrippa had translated repeated themselves over and over in her mind as her fingers fondled the medallion. She was appalled at the thought, and half-believing in the truth of it only made it worse.

She felt the hot sting of tears in her eyes; tears of helplessness and apprehension, and of loneliness. Suddenly she would have given a great deal to be back within the security of that shabby collection of huts and shelters that was her home, back with Brede and the others.

It was true that in the half-world between waking and sleeping she had dreamed of being restored to her real family and her real home; dreamed, even, of being claimed by a handsome stranger on a tall horse, who revealed that she was really the daughter of the king of an important tribe, perhaps in remote northern parts or even across the sea. A queen, indeed. Someone destined to be another Boudicca. Yes, she had had her dreams, for she had been a lonely child. But not like this! Not carelessly lost by some long-gone Roman. Not a Roman's daughter . . . The tears welled up in her dark blue eyes and spilled silently down her pale, too-thin face.

CHAPTER TWO

MUCH later, she stared dismally at the plate of fish and sliced egg that Agrippa had brought and left for her, unable to bring herself to eat it. He had said she would have to remain at the fort overnight and no amount of argument and protest could alter that, and although he said he knew nothing more, she felt that he did know, and that her fate had been decided.

There were still two guards outside the door. Had there been only one she might have contrived to trick him and make a bid for freedom, but two . . . She could not even talk to them to try to persuade them to let her go; they would not understand a word she said. She sighed and supposed she could always set the room on fire with the torch that was in a wall sconce and was the room's only light; but such an action was not very appealing and she did not seriously consider it.

Brede would begin to worry about her as the shadows lengthened. She had optimistically asked Agrippa if someone could go and tell them what had happened to her but he had merely said he was sorry, he could not be spared and there was no-one else. She wondered if the men would go out and search for her in the fading light. More likely they would wait until dawn. If the currents and the breeze had not set the little boat drifting far out into the lake, they might find it and think she had drowned. Even if they did not find the boat, that is what they undoubtedly would assume anyway, and give up their search.

Agrippa came to take away the food she had barely nibbled, ignoring her demands to be taken back to the village. She felt vulnerable and miserable and angry and helpless, and sleep was virtually impossible. She tried to shut out thoughts of whether or not she was the daughter of Pontius Aquila, the Roman, and the twin sister of Marcus and the younger sister of Octavia. She could not even pronounce the names. How could she always have been Roman and not known it? How could she be one half of twins and not ever have felt it?

Yet, it was quite possible, quite feasible. It did have a ring of truth—she could not totally refuse to believe it. It had always been known and understood that she had not been born an Iceni—only never had anyone contemplated that she might have been born a Roman.

She passed a long and lonely night. Between bouts of restless sleep she lay in turmoil, sometimes denying vehemently to herself that she could conceivably be Thelia, and sometimes feeling almost resigned to the fact that it was so.

When Flavius and Agrippa appeared early the following morning, she had resolved nothing. Exhausted, watery-eyed with tiredness, she gave them no more than a glance. Flavius made formal enquiries, through Agrippa, as to her well-being and trusted she had not spent too uncomfortable a night. She did not trust herself to answer civilly, nor to keep her temper, and so took refuge in silence and sat staring at the wall, presenting them only with her expressionless profile.

'You are to go to Rome,' Agrippa said suddenly.

Thea, for a moment, was quite still. Then she turned her head and stared at him, and then at Flavius, who was watching her closely, his dark eyes gleaming. 'Rome?' It came out hoarse and cracked. She swallowed hard and transferred her gaze to Agrippa. 'Rome?' All she knew of Rome was that it was where Romans came from and that it was at the other end of the earth.

'To Pontius Aquila,' Agrippa said, as if by way of explanation. 'You will leave here as soon as I return from your village. Is there anything you wish to take with you from there?'

Just like that? 'I am not going to Rome!' she cried, appalled. She stood up and began to walk towards the door, a proud, determined tilt to her elfin face. Flavius's iron fingers closed on her arm and prevented her. He spoke at some length, and with an almost gentle note in his voice.

'He says,' Agrippa repeated, 'that Pontius and his wife were quite shattered when all attempts to find their daughter failed and they had to return to Rome. The anxiety and the strain left Pontius's wife very ill and she never recovered. She died two years later. Flavius is totally convinced that you are Thelia and feels he has no alternative but to take you to Rome, to Pontius. Even after all this time nothing would mean more to him than to have his daughter restored to him.'

'How does he know that?' she demanded tearfully. 'And what of me? I *am* Iceni. I know nothing of Rome. I cannot speak the language or pronounce the names! I loathe and despise Romans! I do not want to go to Rome even if I am Pontius Aquila's daughter. There is nothing Roman in me. I hate you all. I want to stay here with my friends, among people who have been kind to me—'

Agrippa cut across the tirade with a sharp word and translated what she had said to Flavius, who shrugged his shoulders and said three or four words which Thea did not need interpreted: as far as he was concerned, she would go to Rome and he was not at all interested in her feelings in the matter.

She met his cold eyes with her own angry gaze. 'Well, if you will not care about me, what of him—the Roman? Suppose I am not Thelia? It is a heartless thing to take me there and present me as his daughter and expect him to feel anything. It is too long ago! I am Iceni in every way. How could he possibly see his daughter in me?' She pulled out of his grasp and drew back a little. 'Perhaps he will not wish to have such a daughter, and then what will happen to me? Will I just be left to fend for myself in a strange land so far from everything I know? How shall I get home? What will become of me? Have you spared a thought for that, or do you not care?'

The words had followed one another without any conscious thought behind them, but as Agrippa passed on her protests, she felt herself grow cold. What, indeed, would become of her if Flavius succeeded in forcing her to go to Rome and then Pontius refused to acknowledge her as his daughter? She did not believe anyone would take the trouble to ensure her safe return to these shores. She would be abandoned to her fate.

Tears sprang into her eyes. Flavius, whose gaze had not left her face, took her arm and, not unkindly, led her back to the seat. She sat down and looked up at him, and a tremor slid over her. Something in his eyes completely unnerved her but he spoke gently and there was a degree of kindness in his voice.

Agrippa, however, seemed reluctant to repeat what he said and spoke carefully. 'He says that should things not happen the way he believes they will, he considers that you will be a great deal better off in Rome with some wealthy family than half-starved and frozen in your little hut. So he feels that the best thing he can do for you is to undertake to see that a good price is asked for you so that you will go to a respected family. He gives you his word that he will personally ensure that you only go to a family who are known to treat their slaves and servants well—'

'A slave!' Thea's horrified voice cut across his words as a flood of anger swept away her misery. 'Oh! I see that Flavius will make his purse fat with Roman coins whichever way it turns out! A reward from the rich Pontius if I am accepted as the beloved lost Thelia and a large slave price to stay his tears if I am not! Well, I will not go to Rome, I will *not*!' In one swift, darting movement, she sprang to her feet and threw herself towards the door.

She had opened it sufficiently to glimpse the guards still outside before Flavius and Agrippa could stop her and push the door shut. It took the two of them to hold her. She kicked, scratched, punched, bit and clawed until, in the end, she found herself hauled up off the floor, bruised and shaken and half-naked where her tunic had come apart at the seams. She held it together with one hand and with the other brushed the tangled mass of hair off her face.

One look at the angry glint in the dark eyes of Flavius and the inscrutable, unyielding set of his jaw, and Thea realised defeat. She sagged in his grasp, her knees suddenly giving way beneath her, and a sob of despair escaped her.

Again Flavius drew her back to the seat and pushed her down into it. There was a short silence and then Agrippa said: 'Is there anything you wish to take with you from the village?'

Thea, head bowed and face partly hidden by a veil of hair, could have wept. It had made no difference, any of it. She would have been better served to have saved her energy. She drew a long breath; she would have her chance, sooner or later, and thought with regret of the knife that had fallen in the lake.

Agrippa was waiting for an answer and, pushing back her hair, she raised her head. What was there in that little hut she thought of as home that she wanted? She thought of the two combs that often held her hair in some sort of order. Delicate combs, lovingly carved in wood by an old man with wonderful, unfailing skill and the enviable patience of the old. She thought of the pin she sometimes wore in her tunic that was made from a bone of the largest fish she had ever caught. She sighed deeply. There was nothing else, really, that mattered. She had the medallion, which was the only other thing she had treasured. It made her smile with irony, now, at the thought of how many pretty fantasies she had woven round it and her unknown past.

'Brede will know,' she said.

Agrippa nodded and turned to leave, but as Flavius opened the door, she raised her voice and said, 'I will have my other tunic though, unless you wish to add to my humiliation by keeping me here like this.

Agrippa merely inclined his head and followed Flavius out. Left alone, Thea drew up her knees and rested her chin on them. She had plenty of time to dwell on her plight. She must try to be as calm as possible about it.

Now that she had cause to question it, she was intelligent enough to realise that she hated Romans probably only because she had been brought up to hate them and because they were invaders of a land and conquerors of a people she had always considered hers. She had had, in actual fact, very little close contact with Romans at all and had usually observed them only from a distance or from a safe hiding place. They had always been a part of her life, but always hated and always avoided.

She shivered a little and got up to stretch her legs. As she did so the door opened suddenly to admit Flavius who was followed by half a dozen soldiers. Thea backed against the wall and stared in astonishment. The first carried a platter of food and a jug of water, two more carried between them a wooden plank on which sat a huge bowl of steaming hot water; another held a soft linen cloth and the last a closed wooden box. The food was put down on the small table that stood in a corner, the folded linen on the bed and everything else was set on the floor. At a word from Flavius, the soldiers wheeled round and marched out. It struck her as slightly absurd and she would have laughed had she been in a lighter frame of mind.

She looked across at Flavius. His gaze travelled slowly down over her and a quirk of amusement lifted a corner of his mouth as she clutched the tunic closer against her and pressed herself against the wall, an icy shiver sliding down her spine. 'Go away!' she snapped; but he moved forward and pushed the wooden box towards her with his foot. She glanced down at it, puzzled, then raised her eyes to meet his amused gaze. He said something in a mocking tone, saluted carelessly and went out. She stared after him, a flush warming her cheeks and something unsettling stirring in her stomach.

She bent down to open the box and found inside a tangle of twine, threads and leather strips, and an assortment of needles, clasps and pins: the means to do something about her tunic. Her flush deepened; perhaps Flavius was not, after all, totally insensitive. She surveyed the other things. Food—this time meats and bread—which she did not think she would be able to eat;

hot water to wash with and soft cloth to dry herself on and, lying on top of this, several combs. She was profoundly grateful, and with one eye warily on the door, she stripped off the tunic and spent an hour happily occupied washing away the dirt, soothing the scratches and bruises sustained in her struggle, and restoring some order to her hair. Refreshed and feeling infinitely better, she wound the long, soft cloth around her, tied back her hair and sat down to try to mend her tunic.

As she worked, she found herself thinking that if it were only a question of travelling south to London or some such place to see Pontius, she might not mind quite so much. Then, if Flavius's theory was proven false, she at least would be in Britain and she was resourceful enough to be able to take care of herself.

But Rome . . . She shivered at the thought. To end up a slave in some far-distant land made her feel sick with fear. She tried to picture herself there; tried to imagine how it would be if Pontius did indeed accept Flavius's story and welcomed her 'with joy and thanksgiving', but she found it impossible. Far more likely seemed a future of slavery and misery and the thoughts and pictures that kept presenting themselves to her made her shudder.

The remainder of the day passed slowly. Flavius came back and had everything removed. He regarded the untouched food with a frown of displeasure and stood looking at her for several moments, his unsmiling gaze taking in her mended tunic and tidied hair, and her pallor and thinness, but he went away without a word.

Agrippa returned eventually with a small pile of clothing held in a bundle by a belt; the combs, the fish-bone pin and Brede's own precious copper bracelet. A lump rose in Thea's throat at the sight of it. How undeserving she was of Brede's affection. When she questioned him,

MY DAUGHTER THELIA 29

Agrippa said little of his visit to the village. He and the half-dozen men who had accompanied him had met little resistance and his explanations had been accepted readily enough. Brede had given him everything without question and with hardly a word. Silently Thea cursed them all for their ready belief and unquestioning acceptance. She could expect no help from them.

Agrippa glanced at the still-untouched food and said Flavius had told him to warn her that he would not tolerate her being ill through refusing to eat and would forcibly feed her if necessary. 'He is capable of it,' he said kindly, 'and I would not advise making him do it. You will leave here tomorrow and until you see Maximus you will have only Flavius and an escort for protection. If I were you I should not wish to anger him.'

'Maximus, the Governor?' Thea asked. 'We are to see him?'

'Flavius must gain permission to take you to Rome. If it is given, he plans to take you by ship, if possible. To go over land is quicker, of course, but the risks are too great.'

What he means, thought Thea wryly, is that I should have more opportunity to escape; there is little I can do on a ship. But hope had stirred in her heart. All was not lost. Trebellius Maximus, the new Governor, might well dismiss Flavius's theory and withhold permission.

When she was alone again, she nibbled uninterestedly at the meat and then realised how hungry she was and ate everything. There was boar—that she could identify easily, although it had a delicate flavour of rosemary. But the other—a bird of some type, pheasant perhaps, although if so she wondered what they had done to it to make it so delicious for it fairly melted in her mouth. And who cooked for them? The bread was little different from that she was used to, though it had been spread with honey and sprinkled with the dried flower of heather.

When she had finished, and had drunk deeply of the cool, sweet water, she sat back and delighted in the feeling of fullness, wondering if Romans had such succulent meat on their table all through the winter too, and reflecting that such an amount as she had just eaten would normally have fed both her and Brede.

She took up the bundle of clothing and undid the belt. There was little enough; there had been no need for fancy garments. As she separated the things, a small object dropped out and fell to the floor. She caught her breath and scooped it up in wonder. A knife! It was small but its edges were sharp and it would serve very well. She raised it to her lips and kissed the hilt gleefully. Dear, wonderful Brede! How could she ever have doubted her or thought ill of her!

Alert for any sound from outside, she pulled the binding from her hair, wound the middle of it round the knife hilt and then put it up to her neck and tied the ends beneath her hair at the back. She dropped it inside her tunic and it lay between her small breasts, the blade cool against her skin. She did not dare remove it again in case she did not get a chance to put it back and when she lay down to try to rest, she prayed to the gods to reward Brede well and keep her safe, and she drifted quickly into sleep, happier in the knowledge that the little weapon was there.

When they set off the following morning it was barely light. Thea pulled her woollen mantle around her shoulders against the cool of the early morning as she stepped up into the chariot to stand beside Flavius and the escort of six armed and mounted soldiers gathered around them.

They left the fort behind them and struck out southwards along the straight-hewn road. Despite her fears and her animosity towards the man beside her, Thea could not help a thrill of excitement coursing through her veins as the edges of her mantle licked at the edges of his, and her hair, unconfined by combs or braids, streamed out behind her.

It was a long and trying journey, however, and took two days, with stops every few hours to rest both the horses and themselves. Without Agrippa, Thea was silent and would have found everything extremely difficult except that Flavius anticipated her needs and saw that she was protected from the soldiers; he contrived to allow her all the privacy she needed whilst still guarding her well. She was sure his attentiveness was due only to a concern that she should have no complaints to relate to anyone, and she could not dispel her distrust of him. She slept with the little knife not hidden beneath her tunic but easily to hand, although she had no opportunity to escape and instead had to put her faith in the Governor refusing to give Flavius leave to go to Rome.

It was late when they arrived at the Roman encampment where Maximus was residing. Drooping with tiredness, she was only too willing to allow herself to submit to the ministrations of the two women slaves sent to look after her, although she went to great lengths to keep her knife concealed. When she had washed the grime of travelling from her, and eaten a little, she crawled into a bed thick with soft linen and slept undisturbed until morning.

She was awoken early and hastened through dressing by one of the women, who told her that Maximus had sent for her. Her hair was combed and left loose and when eventually they considered her ready, one of the women held up an oval of pale metal, polished smooth and gleaming, and in it she could see her face quite clearly. After a moment, the woman started to take it away, but Thea put out a hand to stop her and stared long and hard at her reflection. Now that she could see her face without the swaying, watery blur, she was fascinated. Dark red hair in a mass on her shoulders and deep blue eyes in a pointed face. Was she really Thelia? Was there really, in Rome, a boy who looked so much like her that Flavius had recognised her almost immediately?

The woman gently took away the mirror and hurried her, leaving her no opportunity to retrieve the knife from amongst her pile of clothing where she had thrust it out of sight. She was led down several passageways and eventually into a chamber where Maximus sat with Flavius, who seemed quite at his leisure. He looked up as she entered, his eyes hooded and a slow smile creasing his face.

She shot him a glaring look and turned her hopeful gaze on Maximus, who sat back and stared at her. It was something she was becoming used to and she did not flinch beneath his scrutiny but looked steadily back at him. She was beckoned closer and the medallion again examined—she wished she had had the presence of mind to drop it somewhere along the road from the fort. She dared not speak, but listened intently as Maximus spoke to Flavius, catching the words 'Pontius' and 'Thelia' and something that might have been Rome. He nodded several times as if in agreement. She fancied, too, that he knew Pontius Aquila personally, a possibility she had not considered before and from his manner, Flavius also seemed acquainted with the Governor. Her heart sank. Her fate, she realised, had been decided.

As soon as there was a pause in the conversation, she opened her mouth to speak, determined not to give in too easily, but she had barely said two words before Maximus turned a look of disdain upon her and waved her away as if she had suddenly become an irritation. A guard came forward to lead her away, and it did not seem at all wise to struggle or voice her protests. Instead she twisted round and looked pleadingly at Flavius, but he would not meet her gaze and turned away from her.

She was shaking with anger. How dare they treat her like that! Tears of frustration stung her eyes and she brushed them away angrily. She would not give in. She would have an opportunity to escape, sooner or later.

Within an hour she was being hastened to the chariot again, only now the escort was leaving them and returning north. It occurred to her that it would be natural for her to ask for one of the women to accompany her, but since she fully intended to escape, somehow, before very much longer, she did not want more than Flavius to contend with, and since no-one suggested that she should have someone with her, she held her tongue.

As it turned out, the gods were more than generous in presenting her with an opportunity, for as they set off once more, it began to rain, the light misty rain of early summer. Flavius seemed impervious to the discomfort at first and she could only clutch her mantle closer around her and bow her head against it. Eventually, however, the drizzle became a driving penetrating downpour and they turned off the road and took shelter in a wood, drawing to a stop between the trees and under a canopy of leafy branches. She knew she would get no better chance.

When he sprang from the chariot and turned to help her down, she shook her head and sat in the corner where she had been standing and pulled her mantle up over her head against the drips. He shrugged his shoulders and left her there, and she slid her bundle of clothes towards her and felt amongst it for the knife which, to her relief was still where she had left it. With a wary eye on the Roman, she drew it quickly out of sight and sat for a few moments until his back was turned. Then she slipped out of the chariot and ran off into the woods as quickly and as quietly as she could.

He heard her and cursed, and as she ducked beneath low branches and thrust her way through the bushy undergrowth, she could hear him crashing after her. Her heart thudded painfully, brambles and saplings tore at her legs and damp leaves slapped her face as she ran, her mantle catching on thorns and twigs until she unclasped it and let it fall, the only thought in her mind being to get away.

He shouted her name several times, imperious and angry, but she was light and agile and no longer hampered as he was by a heavy mantle. She dodged between tangled shrubs, ploughed through fern and leapt over fallen tree trunks, and the gap between them widened.

Abruptly, the trees gave way to a wide, grassy glade into which the rain fell unhindered through the gap in the branches above, and as she lengthened her stride in anticipation of the even ground, she slipped on the wet grass and fell in a sprawling heap. She lay winded for only a moment before scrambling to her feet, but it was enough for Flavius to catch up with her. He caught at her arm and spun her round and she thrust out at him with the knife. It was an instinctive movement and the awkward angle gave it little power, but it struck a glancing blow and he made a sharp sound and stiffened.

In another moment he had wrenched the knife from her fingers and pulled her hard against him. Forcing her head up he kissed her; a hard, passionless, punishing kiss that left her weak and shaken. When he released her, her stomach was churning and her legs trembling, but he gave her no time to recover. He turned heel and pulled her roughly after him, an angry gleam in his eyes. She gasped at the merciless speed with which he dragged her through the trees, silent, unyielding and with unerring accuracy, back to the chariot, scooping up her sodden mantle as he went.

She stood, shocked and confused, against the trunk of a tree and silently accepted his mantle, which he had taken off and held out to her. It was damp, but hers was wet through and she was soaked to the skin. She was also shivering, but whether due to the rain or to his kiss, she did not know. Her lips felt sore and bruised and she did not understand why he had done it except to punish her, for there had been no passion in it.

Her knife had caught his shoulder and blood soaked through his tunic. She watched him bring under cover the few things that had been in the chariot, and unharness the horses, using his left arm as little as possible. He set her bundle down and rummaged through it looking, she thought, for another weapon. But he extracted from amongst the assortment of things her other tunic and thrust it at her, indicating with an abrupt gesture that she should change. Then he went to sit on a fallen tree trunk, digging her knife up to its hilt in the soft earth at his feet. She thought for a moment that he was going to watch her, but he ignored her and pulled down the neck of his tunic to examine his wound. She moved around to the other side of the tree, stood with her back to it and quickly peeled off the wet garment and donned the other, uncomfortably aware, for those few seconds, that if he cared to glance up, her naked back was only partially hidden from his view.

When she turned back, however, he was seemingly engrossed in tying a knot, with one hand and his teeth, in a strip of cloth which held a pad in place over the wound, staunching the flow of blood. She had no idea whether or not it was serious; his rigid expression had not altered. She did not care. She was angry with herself for being so impulsive and failing in what was probably her only chance to escape. He would guard her even more closely now and she had lost the knife.

By the time the rain eased sufficiently for them to continue, Thea was almost eager to be gone. She had had to force down the food Flavius had given her and it lay heavily in her stomach. She was chilled, her thoughts were in turmoil and she was sure she would scream if she had to bear much more of Flavius's grim silence and the constant sound of dripping rain.

He pushed the pace relentlessly when they set off again and it was drawing towards dusk when they reached a small town on the coast, built by Romans and dominated by the fortress in which they spent the night. By this time Thea ached with tiredness and the strain of the past few days; she had no idea where she was and did not, at that point, really care.

She did not know what Flavius said to the garrison commander but she was treated with great respect and consideration and was again glad to let others deal with her, barely aware of what was happening to her and not caring how many opportunities to escape went by. Eventually, she was put to bed and she fell instantly into a deep sleep.

When she awoke the following morning, she felt strangely dizzy. Her head throbbed and her limbs ached: the effects, she thought, of the long journey and the constant state of tension, fear and suspicion in which she had spent the past days. There was a ship sailing for Rome later that day and Flavius was obviously extremely pleased. Thea was not surprised at his fortune, for the gods seemed to be favouring him at every turn.

She was left much to her own devices and although she knew she should be trying to get away while Flavius was occupied with the details of joining the ship, she had little energy and could not concentrate on anything. Perhaps if Flavius knew she felt unwell, he would not make her go on that ship—but she had little faith in that, and felt that if he was aware of her weakness, it would give him an advantage over her.

She was sure that the aches in her limbs and head were no more than the result of so much travelling and that the shivering and dizziness would pass.

By the time the tide was right for sailing, however, she felt worse. Flavius appeared unaware that anything was wrong. If he noticed her heightened colour and inattentiveness, he probably assumed it was due to silent fury at her inability to do anything about the situation, or preoccupation with schemes for escape which soon would be impossible anyway.

She did not disillusion him. She would go to Rome, for she no longer had any willpower to fight against the inevitability of it. Perhaps it would not be so bad. In any event, it was too late now and it required all her concentration merely to stay on her feet as she followed Flavius towards the ship that would carry her across the seemingly endless sea to her unknown future.

CHAPTER THREE

IT MUST have cost Flavius much money and effort to secure passage on that ship, the mere sight of which would doubtless have terrified Thea as it bumped and shifted on the restless waters, had she been her usual self. But she scarcely noticed and only wondered dully what she had done to deserve such ill fortune for had they been but a day later the ship would have been gone and probably there would not be another for weeks, even months, that was bound direct for Rome. She would have been able to escape then.

As it was, the voyage was a nightmare. Almost as soon as the ship struck the open sea, she began to be sick and this further misery, added to the chill she had caught in the rain, quickly reduced her to a state of wretchedness. There were damp draughts through the flimsy shelters on the deck that served as accommodation, and her inability to keep food down gave her little chance of quick recovery. She gave up any attempt to rise from her pallet and lay alternately shivering and burning beneath the coarse bedding.

As the ship heaved in uneasy waters, her stomach churned mercilessly, and her condition worsened. She grew hotter and hotter yet could not stop shivering and thrashed wildly at the irritating things that covered her and at the hands that tried to calm her. She tried to swallow the stuff that was put to her lips, usually only to

MY DAUGHTER THELIA

return it, with a violent contraction of her stomach, a little later. She cried out for water and for Brede and eventually slipped into delirium, unaware of time and oblivious to her surroundings.

As she tossed and turned in the throes of a raging fever, Thea was carried back and forth in time, swept through a disjointed jumble of the scenes of her life, distorted and unrelated, some vivid and frightening, others misty and vague, sometimes joyful, often sinister.

The medallion grew into a portent of evil in her mind and she became obsessed by it, convinced that her only means to escape death at the hands of the Romans was to throw it into the depths of the sea, thereby releasing her from its evil power.

It took a great effort to raise her arms and undo the leather thong that held the medallion around her neck and when she had it in her hand, she fell back exhausted. It was several minutes before she struggled to rise and she managed to draw on a strength which only feverish obsession could give her. Dizziness swamped her but she clung to the heavy cloth covering the opening until the worst of it passed, and then struggled outside. She leaned dangerously over the swollen turbulence, spray lashing her face and soaking her tunic, with the charm dangling from her fingers.

'Thea!' She was wrenched back with a suddenness and a force that made her gasp and the medallion dropped onto the deck. The face before her was familiar, and she knew it was the cause of her misery. Hatred welled up in her and she struggled in his grasp; but the face swam and blurred and although the mouth formed words, she could not make sense of them. Nausea rose, and she began to lose her grip on consciousness as everything swayed and spun around her, and she collapsed into his arms, the swirling greyness closing in on her and forcing her under.

She was aware of someone removing her stained and sodden tunic and wrapping her in something soft and warm, then she lost all sense of time as she drifted in and out of consciousness and delirium. She did not know how long she lay there, caught up in a force that was willing her to die.

Sometimes, in rare moments of coherence, she was aware of being cradled in strong arms and touched by gentle hands with cool, damp cloths and soothed by murmured words she did not understand. Vaguely, she heard voices raised in anger and violent argument and thought that the motion of the ship had lessened. But it was all such a long way away and concentration required a strength she no longer had. Someone came and gave her a bitter liquid to drink which sent violent shudders all through her and she thought she was being poisoned and had no power to prevent it. Then the rolling of the ship began again and grew worse than ever.

How long she teetered on the brink of death she would never know. But periods of clarity and awareness slowly lengthened and the worst of the fever gradually abated. Unable to do more than sip water without being wracked by sickness, however, she grew no stronger and merely lay silent and still, robbed of energy and devoid of expression.

She was increasingly aware, through the mists that frequently clouded her mind, of Flavius constantly beside her, providing the cloths and water and reassurance. With what little mental strength she had left, she hated him for it. Was it not bad enough that she had to suffer such misery without her pride being completely destroyed too? The thought lay dully in her mind that his only concern was to get her to Rome alive so that he might fill his purse and enjoy the favour of Pontius Aquila. But she was too weak to really care.

Then, at last, the ship ceased to toss like a pine cone in the foaming torrent of a mountain stream, and instead glided gently through smoother waters, and Thea roused herself sufficiently to realise that the chill draughts no longer invaded her shelter and that a glowing warmth had dried the damp hangings and filled the space around her with a subdued golden light.

The curtains parted to admit a smiling Flavius. Thea was instantly aware of a sharp pang of hatred and resentment. She turned her face away, closing her eyes. He seemed to hesitate, then he picked her up, wrapped in her coverings, and carried her outside. The movement made her head swim and she flinched from the sudden stab of glaring light.

'Ostia,' he said. His voice had a gentle persuasion about it and she raised her throbbing head to look at him. He inclined his head towards the shore, and repeated, 'Ostia.' His gaze roamed the scene before him almost hungrily, and there was a sparkle in his eyes that might almost have been excitement. He was home. That much penetrated the numbness of Thea's mind; also that Ostia was not Rome, so the journey was not ended. It was merely a silent statement. She had no strength to feel dismayed.

The effort merely of moving her head cost her dearly but she turned slowly to follow his intent gaze. Wonderous structures rose majestically from a tangled mass of buildings that sprawled along the shore line; the harbour was scattered with ships of every size and shape, and an unbearable hubbub of noise filled the air.

It was only a few moments, and then the clash of

colours, the brightness and heat of the sunlight and the violent cacophony of sound suddenly became intolerable and crushed in on her in a swirling blur of screaming light. Her senses reeled, dizziness overwhelmed her and she turned her head against Flavius's chest, squeezing her eyes shut and letting a shuddering sob escape her. As his arms tightened around her, she sank slowly into darkness and oblivion.

Whether what followed covered hours or days, she did not know. She was only aware of a series of movements and places and people; of strange-tasting liquids and water passing between her lips; of a constant noise everywhere and of Flavius standing over her. It seemed that every time she opened her eyes he was there and her animosity deepened.

When next she awoke to full consciousness, and with the throbbing of her head no longer driving all else from her mind, she was lying in what seemed to her to be a vast room, suffused with a gentle light and pleasantly cool. She let her gaze move slowly round the room, taking in the luxurious hangings, the busts on tall marble columns, the lamps . . . It had the strange splendour of Maximus's villa in Britain. And on the wall was a polished-metal mirror, such as the small one she had looked into there, although this one was very long and narrow and the chinks of golden sunlight from the veiled window were caught and spun in it, making dancing yellow patterns on the ceiling above her.

She wondered where she was. It was very quiet. Perhaps she was no longer in the clamouring noise of Ostia; yet surely it was too quiet to be Rome. Questions came pouring in on her and she closed her eyes against them for she was too tired to think clearly. Her limbs felt leaden and she moved her arm with effort. When she looked down the length of the bed in which she lay, she was shocked that the covers were barely raised over the thinness of her body.

She lay for some time letting her thoughts drift and flushed at the thought of how Flavius had seen her during the voyage. She would never forgive him for making her suffer such horrors, and the fact that she had survived and was alive at least, if not in good health, seemed to her to be a miracle.

'Thelia.' She turned her head. A man in his middle years, with short, straight grey hair, wearing a long robe trimmed with gold and held with a glittering gold clasp at his shoulder, stood smiling at her. 'I am Pontius Aquila,' he said gently, 'your father.' He spoke haltingly in her language, a result no doubt of the years spent in Britain. And despite herself, she warmed to him. His kindly blue eyes were soft with unshed tears. She pulled her arm from beneath the covers and he took her hand in both his and sat beside her on the bed.

There seemed no question that he accepted her as his daughter and she did not know what to say to him. It was too much to think about now. She passed her tongue over her dry lips and swallowed hard; there was a bitter taste in her mouth.

'You are hungry?' Pontius asked, half-rising. 'Thirsty?' She nodded and he patted her hand and went off at once.

When he returned a little while later, a young slave girl bore a tray of bowls and jugs and behind her came two people on whom Thea's attention rested. She did not need Pontius's introduction to the young man: it was like looking at a masculine version of herself. He was taller, his hair was short and his jaw more square. He smiled at her and said something that sounded kind. A strange sensation stirred in her—this was her twin brother.

After a long, silent moment, she drew her gaze away with difficulty and looked at the young woman Pontius said was Octavia. She had the same eyes, but her hair, piled on her head in intricate curls, was darker and she held herself proudly, a little aloof; around her neck she wore the same medallion. She did not smile, but inclined her head slightly. Thea did not feel the same warmth in her that she had sensed in Marcus and her gaze returned to him.

She *was* Thelia. She did not doubt it now. Had she ever, really, doubted it? No wonder Flavius had been so sure. But still he had had no right to bring her here, into their lives. How could she bear it? Would she ever learn their language and their ways, or rid herself of the distrust and dislike of all Romans that she had grown up with? It was all too strange, too much to consider and wonder about.

Unbidden tears of self-pity stung her eyes and she turned her head away to hide them. Pontius, however, was quick to sense her confusion and ushered them all out, softly telling her to sleep.

Left alone again, she lay unmoving for a long while before she realised that the slave girl was still there, sitting quietly in the corner. It reminded her of her thirst and she made an attempt to rise. She could not, of course, and the girl hurried to her side. With her help, Thea sipped the cool water and even managed a few mouthfuls of the bland—but probably nourishing— food. It was barely solid and quite unrecognisable, but she knew she could not have managed anything else. The effort left her exhausted and she lay back and drifted into sleep.

She did little but sleep and eat for three days and sometimes feigned sleep when Pontius or Marcus came to see her so that she would not have the ordeal of facing them. But then Flavius came and stood regarding her silently until she had to open her eyes, knowing he had not been fooled. His mere presence caused her heart to thump and her pulses to race with a strong desire to lash out at him. Did he even realise what he had done to her? Her first glance at her reflection in that long mirror on the wall had been a shock. She now looked nothing like she had looked at Maximus's villa or even in the uncertain reflection in the lake. The ravages of the voyage had left their mark and the deathly pallor, hollow cheeks and dark-shadowed eyes made her look like a stranger. But she was powerless to do anything more than glare at him, which seemed only to amuse him. It did, however, have the effect of rousing her out of her fear of facing what had to be faced.

She was weak, unhappy and lonely in those first days and it was a measure of her inherent toughness and resilience that she recovered so quickly. In a week she was sitting up eating small meals, in two she was able to get out of bed without feeling dizzy and walk around. The barrier of language made everything seem doubly difficult, and she had no strength to deal with the conflicting rush of emotions that beset her every time Pontius looked at her in that fond way, or she looked at Brede's bracelet and thought of home.

But once she was able to sit outside in the shady, secluded garden of the villa which she learned was on the very outskirts of Rome she began, almost despite herself, to take an interest.

She expected questions, but there were none—there was no doubt in the mind of Pontius Aquila that she was his daughter and all he needed to know he had gleaned from Flavius. He brought her a painting one day of her mother Aurelia, and the family likeness was striking. She felt a little sorry for Pontius that his children so clearly took after their mother rather than him. There was a great sadness in his voice as he looked at the picture and said: 'I wish she had lived to see you returned to us.' Although he spoke Latin, Thea could guess the sentiment behind the words and when he looked at her, she wondered if either of them would ever be able to bridge the gulf of the missing years. It must be worse for him, she thought, to look at me, his daughter, and realise that I remember nothing of those early years and cannot even speak his language—worse, that I was brought up to hate and distrust all Romans.

But the strange feelings she experienced in those early days, as she tried to reconcile the years of Iceni upbringing with her true Roman origins, gradually subsided beneath a growing sense of belonging. For the first time that she could remember, Thea was loved. She had a family, her father overwhelmed her with affection and attention and she quickly grew very fond of him, and although Octavia remained a little wary, she had an immediate affinity with Marcus and wondered how she could ever have been ignorant of his existence. It was a new emotion for a girl who had always been 'different', and on the outside of real family affection and security. She was honest enough to admit that there was little, really, to tie her to Brede and the Iceni, and the advantages of being the daughter of Pontius Aquila were not lost on her. Within a very short time, she was left in no doubt that here was luxury and an ease of living she could never even have imagined before.

The villa itself was cool and spacious; the floors were

laid with beautiful mosaics which fascinated her, and the rooms were filled with soft couches, foot stools, long marble-topped tables and bronze figurines and porcelain urns. She wandered through the rooms, touching everything in wonder, marvelling at the softness of some of the fabrics and the silkiness of the stone, asking and memorising the names of the strange and beautiful objects. 'If only Brede could see me,' she thought more than once as she luxuriated in a steaming hot perfumed bath. 'How she would stare!'

The gardens, too, were beautiful—cyprus and peach trees provided shade over stone seats and small ponds and fountains were surrounded by marble statues and shrubs such as oleander and myrtle. Flowers grew in profusion and in such colours that Thea could not help but exclaim over them. To think that she might have lived the rest of her life in ignorance of such beauty!

The food alone was a constant source of amazement and delight to her as she was gradually introduced to the tantalising flavours of pike, stuffed marrow, snails, leeks, lobster, figs and grapes, with the promise of even more exotic delicacies once her father returned to his house in the city and began entertaining again. Then there would be a lavish party to celebrate her homecoming and half the city would be invited. This Thea learned from Marcus, and shivered at the thought of the curiosity of so many important people. She fervently hoped her quiet seclusion at the villa would be prolonged as long as possible to enable her to gain some fluency in the language, and become familiar with the ways and manners of Rome, so that she would not disgrace her father.

As soon as she was strong enough, a tutor was appointed for her—one Cornelius, a man fluent in five languages who was gaunt and wizened and had long, grey hair. At first the short sessions with him in the gardens baffled and confused her so much that she came close to breaking down and weeping like a child at her misery and the unknown ordeals that faced her. As the days passed into weeks, however, the lessons became less terrifying and she began to enjoy them. She was naturally intelligent and possessed not only a grim determination to succeed, but also a keen sense of humour and a healthy curiosity, which carried her through the difficult periods.

She also owed much to a determination to be strong enough to learn the language with fluency, face Flavius and tell him exactly what she thought of his treatment of her. She had only to think of the indignities of the voyage to blush scarlet and tremble with anger, and any thought of his brutal kiss when she had tried to escape from him made her shudder. Fortunately—for him—Flavius had been an infrequent visitor to the villa. He had many old friends to catch up with and business to attend to, and she had caught only fleeting glimpses of him and then invariably managed to escape to the gardens without actually having to greet him, for even at a distance the sight of him had the power to arouse an intense feeling of dislike in the pit of her stomach.

She discarded her tunics as soon as she had filled out enough to have new garments made for her, and the first time she tried on one of her new gowns, Octavia uncharacteristically offered to lend her own servant to dress her hair, although Thea had an instinctive feeling that it was more to avoid being ashamed of the sister who had been foisted on her than any real desire to help her. Her first inclination was to refuse, but she wanted Octavia's friendship and agreed.

MY DAUGHTER THELIA

When she stared at her reflection in the mirror, she could not help a gasp of wonder. It seemed as though someone completely different stared back at her. She was still thin and but for that and the lighter colour of her hair, it might almost have been Octavia who stood there. In the long, pale blue gown with its gold-trimmed bodice, hem and sleeves, her feet clad in delicate sandals, her hair coiled on top of her head and a gold arm band, given to her by her father, encircling her left arm, there was very little there of the Iceni girl whom Flavius had caught on the bank of a moorland lake on a day that seemed an age ago.

'It is not possible,' she said slowly to Octavia, her gaze not wavering from the vision before her.

Octavia stood back and surveyed her critically. 'Why, you are quite beautiful,' she said in some surprise, but Thea was too preoccupied to wonder about the strange expression that had stolen onto her sister's face.

The effect on Pontius brought an uncomfortable blush to Thea's cheeks. 'Thelia, my Thelia!' he cried, holding her at arm's length before hugging her against his chest. 'How beautiful you look! Now you are truly my daughter again! Soon we will go to Rome and show you off to all our friends!'

Later that day she sat with Marcus in the shady garden waiting for Cornelius; she had laughingly given up trying to explain in Latin how she had spent the years with the Iceni and they had lapsed into companionable silence, until Marcus leaned back and regarded her in some amusement. 'Flavius will hardly be able to call you "little savage" now, you look so civilised.'

She looked at him enquiringly and he repeated his remark more slowly. 'What is sa-vage?' she asked carefully in Latin. Marcus chuckled, but instead of trying to explain, gestured towards Cornelius who was walking towards them and told her to ask him. Before she could argue, he got up and left her to her lessons. Cornelius, when questioned, looked at her out of sharp eyes and explained the word briefly in her own language, bringing a gasp of indignation to her lips.

So he thought she was a savage, did he? And no doubt went about saying so to half Rome! How dare he—? Her eyes gleamed with anger but Cornelius called her sharply to attention and she had to drag her thoughts back to her lessons. Incensed, her attention that afternoon was erratic and Cornelius had several times to reprimand her; but she was left with a greatly increased determination. The sooner she could tell Flavius how she despised him, in terms he could clearly understand, the better. And no-one, least of all Flavius, should have any cause to call her a savage.

Finally, the pleasant sojourn in the villa was brought to an end. Pontius declared that evening that they would return to Rome at the end of the week and at the same time announced a date for the celebrations in Thea's honour—only two weeks later. Thea's face must have shown her dismay, for he smiled tenderly at her. 'You must not worry. You are strong now and everyone will make allowances.'

'I do not wish to—to disappoint you,' she said haltingly. 'I think—I think it will be difficult.'

'Nonsense!' Marcus laughed. 'It will be fun and we will all be there to rescue you. No doubt Flavius will be at the centre of it all anyway, to steal the attention for having been the one to find you and bring you home!'

'You'll have to meet the rest of the family and our friends sooner or later,' Octavia said. 'Better to get it over with all at once.'

'Octavia, really,' Pontius reprimanded her gently.

'We will be able to show you the city at last,' Marcus continued with boyish enthusiasm. 'There is so much to see.'

Thea's dismay that the party was to be so soon vanished beneath a smile. Marcus had already excited her imagination with descriptions of the city and she had an endless list of things he wished to show her. She could not help but feel excited at the prospect.

The remainder of the week passed swiftly. Conscious of the impending ordeal of meeting innumerable people and having to carry on some kind of conversation with them, Thea's attention to her lessons became almost an obsession and she began even to dream in Latin.

At the end of the week, the family packed their personal effects into the carriage and, with what seemed to Thea to be a small army of servants and slaves and a hoard of vegetables, fruit, wines and meats from the surrounding countryside, they left the tranquillity of the villa and journeyed to the house in the centre of Rome.

It was almost as large as the country villa and Thea's bedroom had a lovely view over the garden which, though smaller than the villa's was attractive and pleasant, dotted with statues and cyprus trees and separated from its neighbour by a high wall covered with vines.

The painting of her mother had been brought from the villa and hung by Pontius above the bed. On the opposite wall a mirror, this time in an elaborate golden frame and if possible even more highly burnished and gleaming than the one in her room at the villa, reflected a younger face with an unmistakable likeness, as Thea stared at herself and wondered how long it would be before she could do so without being surprised at what she saw. 'I am Roman,' she told herself, 'I have a family. We are wealthy and I can have anything I want. I shall never fear the winter again and I shall always have too much to eat—not just enough but too much! Oh, Brede, you would not believe the food . . . And Octavia thinks I am beautiful, beautiful . . .' A smile lit up her face and she twisted away from the mirror and danced across the room.

Marcus came in search of her a little later, with the news that he had obtained their father's permission to show her part of the city with the proviso that if they insisted on walking rather than travelling more properly by litter, they must have two of the household servants accompanying them. 'Walking *is* the only way to see the city properly,' Marcus said, 'and Octavia wishes to make a few purchases, so rather than send for the merchants to come here, she says she will come with us and get what she wants herself. Say nothing to Father, though; he would turn purple at the thought!'

Her first stroll in the sunlit streets of Rome was a revelation. Having lived most of her life in villages and makeshift encampments, the noise and teeming bustle of the city was overwhelming and she gazed around her with eyes wide and lips slightly parted in wonder.

'The forum,' Marcus said, as they walked beneath an elaborate arch into a vast area surrounded by magnificent buildings where all of Rome seemed to have gathered to go about its daily business. 'That is the Temple of Vesta,' he said, pointing to a circular temple with a conical roof, 'and that next to it is the House of the Vestal Virgins who tend the sacred fire—'

'—and have the best places reserved for them at the Games and festivals,' Octavia added.

'And that's the Senate House where Father has to go,

and where all the debates are held and decisions made.' There were other temples too, such as those of Saturn and of Romulus . . . and all around were columns and statues and hundreds of people. They stood in groups engaged in heated discussion, or sat on the steps of the temples or gathered around the fountains talking and laughing; many seemed merely to be strolling through while slave-borne litters paused to disgorge their passengers. Marcus and Octavia seemed to know half Rome. They nodded to many of the people who passed and others called greetings, while some paused to talk. Thea was introduced to countless people, some evidently friends, some dignitaries. She blushed, acutely aware of the curious looks, and murmured the only words of greeting she knew, and as soon as they had moved on, she promptly forgot both the names and the faces.

'That is the Rostra,' Octavia said, indicating a large gathering of people ahead of them. A series of terraces rose up at the foot of what Marcus said was the Capitol. Two or three people were standing on various parts of the terraces holding court to the groups that had gathered around them to listen. Marcus drew his sisters to one side and they paused for a few minutes to listen to one of the speakers.

Thea did not know what he was shouting so earnestly but the crowd were interrupting with bursts of laughter and shouts of derision, though they seemed to be good natured enough. 'These are public speaking platforms,' Marcus explained. 'Anyone can come and speak. This fellow is mad—he wishes everyone in Rome to give up going to the baths because it is sinful and Rome will be destroyed by our evil ways!'

They moved on. Octavia, scornful of the protests of the servants, drew them away to the basilica, a vast building oblong in shape with tall columns around a roofed market place. Thea was enthralled and trailed after her brother and sister lingering at every stall and vendor. Pontius had given her an allowance the same as Marcus and Octavia but she had been at a loss to know what she could possibly want that she did not already have and the sesterces had remained unspent. Now, however, she was presented with an almost awe-inspiring range of goods and trinkets that both fascinated and bewildered her.

'Marcus—look, it's Drusus and Ursula!' Octavia exclaimed and hailed the couple. The four of them were quickly engaged in animated conversation, their servants also unobtrusively conversing together. Thea, relieved that they seemed to have forgotten her, wandered a little way off to look at a colourful display of cloth that had caught her eye, unnoticed by the gossiping attendants. If she had to be introduced to anyone else that day, she thought, she would scream. As she moved away from them, however, a haunting, melodic sound attracted her attention to a small crowd that had gathered around a man who was demonstrating a strange instrument. An assortment of others lay at his feet and Thea listened enchanted as he played, then watched as he haggled the price and eventually sold it to an eager young man who carried it off gleefully.

A harsh screech made her jump and she turned round to see what had made it, and was drawn spellbound towards another small crowd, in the midst of which was a man with a bird. She slipped between the people to the front and what she saw took her breath away. It was the largest, most beautiful bird she had ever seen, with feathers of such vivid blues, reds and yellows that she could only stare at it in wonder. Despite the size of its beak and claws, it seemed quite harmless as it perched on the man's leather-protected arm. How wonderful it would be to own such a creature as that, she thought, and wondered if Pontius would allow her to have one. She was too timid to ask how much it cost, however, but as she stood there a little longer she realised that the man did not intend to sell it and had evidently only brought it to the basilica to show it off. She knew she should return to Marcus and Octavia but could not drag herself away.

Eventually, she turned reluctantly away; as she did so, the bird lifted its gaudy wings slightly and, with an ear-piercing shriek, made a sudden lunge at Thea, its formidable beak missing her arm by inches. With a fearful cry, she fell back into the crowd, her arms raised to fend it off, but the creature was already sitting quietly back on its owner's forearm, head cocked, regarding her malevolently from a small round eye. The people around Thea were laughing and she ducked her head and pushed her way through them, emerging scarlet-faced and tearful, and feeling exceedingly foolish.

She returned to the place where she had left Marcus and Octavia and was horrified to find that neither they nor the servants were there. Cursing herself for having wandered away from them, she spent a few minutes walking around the basilica scanning the faces, but without success. They would wait for her outside, of course, since it was clearly impossible to find anyone among so many people. So, fully expecting to find them waiting for her, she made her way out into daylight.

Her heart sank, for there was no sign of them. Trying to remain calm she walked slowly along the row of columns, whose afternoon shadows had lengthened, scanning the surrounding area and groups of people anxiously.

She was back where she started from, and forced herself to think clearly. She would never be able to find her own way back to the house once she was beyond the forum. The market was the last place Marcus and Octavia had seen her so this was where they would look for her and this was where she should stay until someone came. Surely they would send one of the servants to search the area outside.

A group of unsavoury-looking young men was watching her and she grew increasingly nervous, watching them fearfully and at the same time frantically searching for some sign of Marcus and Octavia, or at least a familiar face. Oh, what a fool she was to have been so easily distracted by a pretty tune and a ridiculous-looking bird . . .

CHAPTER FOUR

'Is anything wrong?'

She spun round, startled, and stared blankly at a man dressed in tunic and sandals with black hair and almost black eyes who was looking enquiringly at her. He had a small scar along one cheek bone. 'I'm sorry,' he said. 'I did not mean to frighten you, but you seem upset . . .'

Thea recovered her composure. 'No. I am waiting,' she said slowly, 'for my brother.' And then, for protection, she added: 'I am the daughter of Pontius Aquila.'

He looked at her for a moment, then smiled, slipping into what she regarded as her native tongue. 'You must be the lost daughter from Britain!'

She suddenly relaxed and dropped the painstaking Latin with great relief. 'I am Thelia, yes, but how do you know about me?'

'Half Rome knows about you. You are quite a heroine—and the noble Flavius will probably have a statue erected in his honour!' Thea grimaced and he chuckled. 'My name is Gryffgar, but no Roman seems able to pronounce it properly so I am Gregor to most. And now that you are not so frightened of me, why were you in such a panic just now?'

The frown returned to her face. 'It is my own fault. I came here with Marcus and Octavia, and was distracted in there—' she indicated the building behind her, 'and stupidly wandered away from them. Now they have disappeared and there is no sign of the servants and I do not know if I can find my way back alone.'

'That is easily righted,' he said, 'Come, I know where Pontius Aquila's house is and I have to go that way.'

She hesitated, chewing her lip. It did not occur to her to distrust the man; merely the sound of a familiar language had sent all thought of caution out of her head. But she did not want to miss Marcus and Octavia. She looked around worriedly. 'Perhaps I should stay here.'

He shrugged his broad shoulders. 'As you wish. But I am late and I shall have to go.'

'Then I will come with you,' she said, having no great desire to linger there alone.

'Why are you in Rome?' she asked him as they walked, 'you are not—a slave?'

'Not now, no. But neither am I here by choice! I began as a slave a few years ago, but I caused a lot of trouble and I was passed on to a gladiator trainer. Now I am a gladiator.'

'Oh.' It explained the scar on his face. 'Do you enjoy it?' she asked doubtfully. She knew little about gladiators, but what she did know—men fighting for the amusement of a crowd—seemed rather gruesome.

He gave a short laugh and looked at her sideways. 'I do not. I have scars all over my body and I have come close to death several times. But few of us actually have to die now; it's not often the crowd demands death. Victory is usually enough. Sometimes someone is killed during the fight, but that,' he shrugged, 'is unfortunate . . . It is a slightly better existence than being a slave.'

Thea doubted it, and was silent for a moment. 'But you have the freedom to come and go as you please?'

'Yes. Tibelius trusts me, the fool.'

'Then why do you not leave?'

MY DAUGHTER THELIA   59

'And go where? I am as tied to Tibelius as a slave when it comes to leaving. As long as he thinks I am happy, I have a reasonable amount of freedom and I can listen and watch and wait. And as soon as I can safely get a passage on a ship going to Britain—or anywhere near Britain—I will. But they are not so frequent and it is not so easy to do without betrayal. If I have to die I would rather it were in the amphitheatre.'

Thea, somewhat disturbed, said nothing for a few minutes and allowed him to guide her down a narrow side street. 'How do you know you can trust me?' she asked at last. 'You have only known me a few minutes.'

Gregor smiled. 'How could anyone so young and lovely even think of betraying a confidence—especially that of a fellow Briton.' She did not argue the point. Uncertain how to treat his words, she gave the shadow of a smile and avoided his eyes. 'Look,' he said, slowing his steps and indicating the street ahead. 'Do you know where you are now?'

She did, and within a few moments they were standing in the shadow of the garden wall. 'Thank you,' she said. 'I should never have found it myself.'

He smiled and shrugged. 'I am often down there, although I admit I seldom have the pleasure of such enchanting company! Perhaps you might lose your escorts again one day.' And with that ambiguous statement and an infectious grin, he left her and sauntered off down the street.

Almost immediately as she turned in towards the house, her arm was caught by iron fingers and she uttered a startled cry. She was wrenched round to find Flavius glaring at her. 'What do you think you are doing?' he demanded, obviously furious; his dark eyes gleamed and his mouth was set in a hard line. 'Do you know what that man is? He is a gladiator. You are the daughter of Pontius Aquila and you are walking around Rome with a common gladiator! Your father is sick with worry, Marcus has gone back to search for you, Octavia is in tears, the servants have been punished . . .'

Thea trembled as he shook her. Her Latin had deserted her, and she stood staring at him, unable to defend herself, understanding barely half of what he said and conscious of pain as his fingers tightened their cruel grip on her arm. Then, suddenly, he was still, the anger fading from his eyes. His gaze slid slowly down over her in a way that left her feeling he could see straight through the flimsy garments she wore. She had no power to pull herself away and her legs were weak and shaking.

After a long, uncomfortable moment, his gaze returned to her face. 'My compliments, my dear Thea,' he said slowly, his grip on her arm relaxing. 'You have become quite beautiful. No longer the pathetic little savage I found on the moor. The transformation is quite—breathtaking.'

Thea wrenched free, the word 'savage' leaping out at her from the jumble of other words only half understood. 'I am *not* a savage!' she snapped. 'How dare you say it! You are a—a—' All the words she had so studiously sought out and memorised for the sole purpose of repeating them to Flavius, suddenly deserted her. 'Oh, I hate you!' she cried in frustration, and would have spun away, except that he caught her and pulled her back, drawing her into his arms. He kissed her fiercely and hungrily, heedless of her rigid, unyielding body straining away from him. The instant he released her, her hand flew up and struck his face a stinging blow. Then she turned and fled to the house.

Much later, when the fuss about her disappearance had died down and the lectures about having anything to do with the likes of gladiators were over, Thea escaped to her room. She closed her eyes, and sighed in relief and thought how good it was to be alone. Her dislike of Flavius had deepened to the extent where the mere thought of him set her shaking with anger. How dared he kiss her like that? Oh, if only she could talk to him as fluently as she had talked to Gregor, what truths she would tell him about himself and his self-satisfied air of importance!

She lay on the bed and stared at the ceiling, not seeing it, shutting out Flavius and thinking of her chance encounter with Gregor. How good it had been to speak fluently and easily again, without having to think about every word or search for the means to express herself properly. It would, she thought, be very pleasant to have at least one friend in all Rome with whom she could talk like that. Someone, too, with whom she could talk about the familiar things of her past without fear of being laughed at or being thought an ignorant savage.

But she would probably now be unable to speak with Gregor even if she should meet him again. Clearly it was forbidden to associate with such lowly characters and no doubt Marcus and Octavia and an army of servants would keep close by her in future.

But she had little time to dwell on thoughts of Gregor in the two weeks that followed. She avoided Flavius, spoke, thought and dreamed in Latin and had two more outings in the city with Marcus, this time quite properly in litters, once to the Circus where chariot races and Public Games were held and once to the amphitheatre where gladiators fought. And, of course, the preparations for the Celebration took a great deal of everyone's time.

The two weeks passed at an alarming pace and the dreaded day arrived. Servants and slaves ran hither and thither, Pontius and Octavia between them supervising the arrangements, and Marcus eventually disappearing completely. Thea wandered the house aimlessly trying to be useful but only succeeding in getting in the way.

Finally, she retreated to her room and amused herself trying on the beautiful new gown she had especially for the occasion, convinced that as soon as one of the guests said anything to her she would blush scarlet and dry up, her scanty knowledge of her new language and the carefully-learned phrases deserting her as completely as they had done when she had faced Flavius.

A measure of satisfaction came to her when, fully dressed, she stood before the mirror and examined her reflection critically. She could find no fault with her appearance. The weight of her hair, piled up and curled, and threaded with blue silk ribbon deliberately chosen to match perfectly the colour of her eyes and the threads in the trimmings of her white gown, naturally drew her head back so that there was a proud tilt to her chin. Boudicca herself had never looked so stately, so beautiful. She wore the gold band her father had given her on one arm, Brede's copper bracelet on the other, and delicate white and gold sandals on her feet. She knew how well she looked, and with that knowledge came confidence.

When she was finally satisfied that she was ready, she sent away the slave girl who had been attending her and went in search of her father to seek his approval, hardly daring to move her head for fear of dislodging the curls or the ribbons.

MY DAUGHTER THELIA 63

A few of the city's most skilled musicians, appointed by Pontius to entertain his guests for the evening, had arrived and were already playing fitfully; pitchers were filled with wine and the long tables were being covered with food.

She found her father in the gardens, which had been adorned with decorations and candle-lamps for the occasion, and went eagerly forward. 'Father—' she began and then stopped abruptly as she realised that he had someone with him, and that it was Flavius. Suddenly a little of the elation and the excitement vanished beneath the instinctive ill-humour that his presence always seemed to arouse in her. But she recovered quickly, forced a shadow of a smile and turned to her father. 'Is it good?' she smiled. 'Do I look nice?' and turned carefully around. When she had turned full circle, Pontius nodded and smiled broadly. 'Daughter, you look lovely. You look like your mother when she was very young. I shall be proud of you tonight, Thelia, and Nero will envy me my daughter.'

Thea went pale. 'Nero?' she murmured. 'The Emperor is coming?' She no longer hated Romans, or believed that they were *all* as evil, cruel and bestial as the Iceni had taught her. Yet Nero had a reputation that seemed to epitomise everything she had been brought up to believe of them, save perhaps that they ate children on feast days, and the thought of meeting him in person unnerved her.

Flavius, who until now had been silent, regarding her with a faintly amused expression, looked at Pontius with a slight frown creasing his brow. 'You did not warn Thea he was coming? Was that wise? The poor child will be terrified, and there is hardly time to prepare her for it.'

'My dear Flavius,' Pontius said smiling, 'Thelia is

quite able to deal with such exalted persons. Do you think she would disgrace us? I have more faith in her.' He patted Thea's hand and gazed indulgently at her. 'And there will be others,' he added returning his gaze to Flavius, 'to divert our lusty Emperor's attention away from her.'

She did not like to hear herself talked about, especially by Flavius and especially when he referred to her as a child. She turned a cold look upon him and with a proud tilt to her chin, turned away and walked slowly back inside with all the dignity she could muster.

The evening was both a trial and a triumph. Certainly a triumph for Pontius in every possible way. And the food—Thea had been promised exotic delicacies and they were here in abundance. Snails, lobster and crab; kid, boar, sucking pig and hare; capon and pheasant, vegetables of every description and bowls of figs, cherries, grapes and nuts. And crowning the table was an osterrich, steaming in a mysterious sauce, the very smell of which made Thea's mouth water, and surrounded by leeks and tomatoes with grapes and herbs.

But for Thea it was every bit the ordeal she had thought it would be, and it had begun even before the first guests arrived. Octavia had appeared, startlingly beautiful in a gown of pale green, with emerald green silk shimmering at the hem and decorating the bodice, crossing between her breasts and forming a band beneath them. She wore a bracelet of gold and jade, and an emerald at her throat and Thea looked pale beside her.

'She has done it deliberately, to outshine you,' Marcus said, outraged for his twin. 'She really is a spiteful, conceited—'

'It is not important,' Thea said quietly, her initial hurt

dulling a little beneath the consoling thought that perhaps if the attention of at least some of the guests was diverted to Octavia, she herself might have a less harrowing evening.

But before the evening was even half way through, her temples throbbed and her head was spinning with names and faces she knew she had very little hope of remembering. She had stood beside her father with Marcus and Octavia to greet the guests as they arrived. 'How good of you to come,' Pontius Aquila exclaimed a hundred times. 'This is my daughter, Thelia . . .' She murmured the right words at the right time and helped by Pontius and Marcus managed to answer the inevitable questions conscious of the curious, penetrating looks and speculative glances.

The Emperor, resplendent in glittering robes, arrived at last and stood in the doorway of the great room surveying the throng. A hushed stillness fell, and Thea's heart began to pound as her father took her arm and guided her towards him to be presented, the other guests drawing back to allow them through. Acutely embarrased at the silence that had descended, she trembled in trepidation. Pontius spoke a few words of formal greeting and then drew her forward.

'. . . and I am proud to present my daughter, Thelia, whom we had thought lost to us many years ago, and whom the gods in their mercy have restored to me to bring me joy and comfort in my old age.'

Thea, as she had been told, dropped gracefully to one knee, head bowed, to be raised immediately to her feet by the warm firm hand of Nero. She lifted her eyes to his and found him smiling. 'Thelia, daughter of Pontius and of Rome, we welcome you back into your father's house. We have a gift—' He gestured one of his attendants forward and presented Thea with a small, yellow bird in an ornate golden cage.

Surprised and enchanted, she glanced at her father, who nodded encouragingly, and she accepted the gift with a delighted smile, gazing at the bright, fluttering bird in wonder. 'It's beautiful,' she murmured, 'Thank you so much. I am honoured.'

Nero waved aside the thanks, laughing. 'Your daughter is charming,' he said to Pontius, 'and you were right to sing her praises to me so highly. She is quite exquisite and the image of your dear Aurelia. Ah, Flavius—' Thea had not noticed him standing to one side, but he stepped quickly forward now as Nero's roving eye took in Thea's young and slender figure, and received official thanks and praise for what he had done. Thea realised that he was no stranger to the Emperor and, indeed, seemed on almost familiar terms. If he only knew how Flavius treated me to get me here, she thought darkly, and watched as Nero put one arm across the shoulders of Pontius and the other, similarly, across those of Flavius and demanded to be led to the wine. 'We will speak again later,' he said to her over his shoulder as they turned away.

Thus dismissed, Thea gratefully handed the golden cage to one of the servants who had come forward to relieve her of it. Now that the formal greetings were over, she slipped gratefully into her seat beside Octavia, cursing the pretty Roman sandals for pinching her feet so. The ladies sat, the men reclined on couches, the musicians resumed their playing and the servants began hurrying about with platters of food and jugs and goblets of wine.

Seated beside Octavia, Thea felt awkward and shy and somehow out of place; the elder girl did nothing to alleviate her difficulties and allowed her to struggle with the rudiments of Latin and monosyllabic answers while she made witty, brilliant conversation with those nearest to her, gay and charming and apparently oblivious to her young sister's uneasiness.

Thea watched her, half envious of her ability to be that way and half resentful that she should go out of her way to be like it on an evening that was essentially her own. She found herself watching Flavius, too, and was not blind to the number of times his eyes strayed across the room to Octavia. She took refuge in the wine. It gave her idle hands some occupation and the servants were very attentive—no sooner was her goblet empty than one or other of them filled it again.

When the tables of food were ravaged, the servants breathless and the guests all flushed with wine, Nero grew bored with formality and rose from his couch to announce his intention of strolling in the garden for some evening air. This acted like a signal for the other guests and as the Emperor summoned Pontius and one or two others to accompany him, people rose and shifted their positions and the noise of conversation and laughter rose markedly. Thea stole the opportunity to excuse herself, and slipped quietly into the comparative quiet of the hall.

Half hidden by a bust of Claudius on a marble column, she leaned back against the wall and relished its coolness on her back. She had the taste of wine in her mouth and grimaced, regretting drinking so much. There was a gnawing emptiness in her stomach for, despite the many dishes the servants had brought to tempt her, she had eaten nothing that evening, her appetite deserting her with the arrival of the first guests.

As she stood there, she began to feel decidedly dizzy

and faintly nauseous as the sparkling sounds of laughter and conversation and music mingled in what seemed to her to a discordant clatter. The room, the people, the lights all began to blur and swim and she closed her eyes against it.

There was a hand on her arm and a voice saying, with a quiet firmness, 'Come with me. You need some fresh air.'

She did not protest and allowed Flavius to lead her unhurriedly to the cool, fragrant air outside. The Emperor had evidently grown tired of strolling for the garden was deserted and he led her to a seat beside a statue of a young boy whose tilted jug trickled water into an oval pool and pushed her down, holding her head until, the dizziness subsiding, she thrust his hand away.

'I am better now,' she murmured, hoping he would go away. He did not. He sat beside her and said: 'What happened?'

'Nothing,' she said. 'I feel—felt—unwell.'

'You drank too much wine and you have eaten hardly anything.'

'Have you watched me all evening?' she demanded, resentfully.

'Of course. You are very beautiful tonight. I apologise for doubting that you could meet Nero without making a fool of yourself. You obviously made a good impression.'

'Am I not a savage now, then?' she asked with an edge to her voice.

The corner of his mouth twitched in amusement but in the darkness she did not notice it. 'I did not say you were not a savage—you have been a savage for too many years and a few months of civilisation will not cure you!'

Fury blazed suddenly in her eyes and she sprang to her

feet. 'I understand many of the things you say now! How dare you say I am a savage, you despicable cur? You are a hateful, worthless, loathsome pig and—'

He caught her arm and pulled her towards him as he stood up to face her. 'Who taught you such pretty words, you delightful child? Not the worthy Cornelius surely? Have you been practising them especially for me? I am honoured.'

'I hate you!' she cried furiously, 'I hope my father gave you plenty of rewards for me after I was so much trouble to you! You are lucky I did not die on the ship. Then you would have nothing!'

'Be quiet, Thea! This is not the time for petty quarrels and rehearsed speeches!' He looked down at her and suddenly smiled disarmingly. 'You are even more lovely when you're angry, you know.' He drew her swiftly towards him, bent his head and kissed her, his hand at the back of her neck forcing her mouth on to his, his other hand at the small of her back pressing her against him. She struggled in vain. His mouth grew insistent and searching and his hand moved slowly from her back upwards to her shoulder and lingered there, caressingly, before moving downwards to the swelling above the low neck of her gown. She stiffened and strained away from him, only to feel his hand slip down between their bodies and over the fullness of her small, rounded breast.

She gasped, afraid of the sudden shivering sensations that engulfed her, and wrenched herself free of his already slackening grip. 'I wish I had killed you with that knife!' She almost spat the words at him, then turned and began to walk quickly away, only to have him catch her and spin her round into his arms before she could do anything about it.

'I should have punished you properly for that, you

little wildcat,' he murmured, and kissed her again, his arms holding her close against him, heedless of her rigid, unyielding body as she fought the treacherous warmth that tingled in her veins. As he released her, her strange emotions gave way to anger and she swiftly raised her arm to slap him. But he caught her hand easily and, holding her gaze with his dark eyes that seemed to mesmerise her, turned it palm upwards. Slowly, so that time seemed to her to stand as still as her heart, he kissed her fingers gently in a sensual gesture that sent shivers all over her.

The suspended moment snapped suddenly, and she snatched her hand away with a gasp and spun round, half-running towards the gaiety of the house, willing him not to follow, and trembling visibly.

'Goodness, Thelia! Whatever have you been doing—' Octavia's voice was a little brittle, perhaps with too much wine and too much flattering attention.

Thea's already flushed face burned as she sat down again, her heart thudding painfully. 'Oh! I—I feel a little unwell. I thought—outside it is cool . . .'

'You were outside a long time with Flavius,' her sister commented, deftly restoring order to a few of Thea's curls which had become loose. 'I hope he behaved himself.'

Confused, and startled that Octavia had been watching her so closely, Thea looked questioningly at her, still trembling slightly. 'I do not understand.'

'Oh, yes you do,' Octavia laughed softly. 'Cornelius told Father that you have a remarkable, natural aptitude for language, and I am quite sure you understand far more than you would like us to think.'

Thea was about to protest when Flavius appeared in the doorway and Octavia's expression and manner sud-

MY DAUGHTER THELIA

denly changed. Putting a cool hand on the younger girl's arm, she said with a sweet smile and a far pleasanter tone, 'Come, have you tasted the osterrich yet?' She summoned a servant. 'You really should, it's quite delicious . . .'

Thea wished the evening was over. She did not understand Octavia's strangely taut voice, and was hurt by her accusation. And Flavius's actions in the garden had left her shaken and disturbed, afraid for the first time of herself and the emotions he so easily stirred up within her, not only anger and dislike but a kind of fear that was almost excitement. She dismissed the thought instantly—he was quite intolerable and the next time he tried to kiss her, she would certainly tell her father how much he was annoying her.

Comforted by that thought, she contrived to put him to the back of her mind and endure the rest of the evening. Octavia remained solicitous and attentive now, though whether it was to protect her from Flavius or to impress her with the number of young men seeking her attention, Thea did not care to guess. She merely wished the ordeal was over and she could go back to her room, take off the wretched sandals, let the slave girl pamper her protesting feet and finally go peacefully to sleep.

CHAPTER FIVE

IT WAS Octavia's suggestion, a week later, that they should go once again to the market place. Pontius was at the Senate, Marcus was riding out of the city with his friends and she was bored. Thea, by this time, had discovered books and was painstakingly learning to read in Latin, although her twin had unceremoniously told her that she was insane to take on such an exercise when she could not even speak the language fluently. But she found that time hung heavily sometimes and she was glad of so absorbing a task to fill the idle hours when everyone else seemed to have so much to do, and it kept her mind from continually drifting into thoughts of Flavius and the episode in the garden.

On that particular day, however, she was not making any progress at all; with a slight breeze drifting in through the window by which she sat, and the twitterings and flutterings of the little yellow bird proving too much of a delightful distraction, she willingly agreed to go out in the city with Octavia.

They rode in litters to the Forum, where Octavia alighted, instructing Thea to do the same, and told the slaves to wait for them. If nothing else, Thea had to admire her sister's courage—she knew well enough that Pontius was horrified at the liking his offspring seemed to have for walking about the city and insisted they always had servants with them if they intended leaving

MY DAUGHTER THELIA

the protection of the litters. Octavia, however, seemed to be able to do as she pleased with impunity and Thea was happy enough to be free of the ever-present attendants.

It was impossible to walk through the vast, teeming area of the Forum without meeting at least a dozen acquaintances, either strolling with servants in tow or peering from litters. Since the party, Thea now knew most of the people they met at least by sight and their oft interrupted progress was actually quite enjoyable.

'Flavius is joining us at dinner this evening,' Octavia remarked casually as she held a length of cloth against her and examined it critically.

'Oh?' Thea murmured, 'Father did not say.' She had no intention of allowing Octavia to know how she felt about Flavius, but her heart sank at the thought.

'Tell me, Thelia,' Octavia continued, as they moved out into the bright sunlight. 'Are you truly glad he brought you back from Britain? You never say, and he does seem to treat you very warily—almost as though he feels some sense of guilt.'

Thea frowned, a little startled. It was unlike Octavia to be so direct and personal. Perhaps she had not fully understood. A slight touch on her arm saved her from having to find an answer, however, and she turned to find the gladiator, Gregor, beside her.

'Gregor!' She had scarce given him a thought since he had escorted her home that day, but could not deny a little flush of pleasure at the sight of him.

'My lady Thelia. I trust you are well.'

'Thelia, I have just seen Livilla,' Octavia said pointedly. 'I shall be back in a few minutes.' She lowered her voice, 'Go over there in the shadows where you cannot so easily be seen—and don't wander off!'

Thea smiled her gratitude at her sister's surprising charity and moved away a short distance with Gregor, who dropped immediately into his native language. 'You have been warned about speaking to me, I see,' he said, seeming rather amused by the fact.

'Yes, but it does not matter,' she answered, with rather more assurance than she felt.

'I hope you enjoyed your evening at the hands of Rome's richest citizens? It was a great success, by all accounts.'

'How—?' she began, then stopped, and smiled a little. 'I forgot, gladiators know everything. Yes, it was a great success. The Emperor gave me a little bird as a gift.'

'Then you are honoured indeed.'

Unsure whether or not he was laughing at her, she said nothing for a moment; then, 'Have you had any luck finding a ship to take you home?'

He shook his head. 'These things take time,' he said vaguely, 'and I cannot afford to take risks.'

'I wish I could help you,' she said, and could not prevent the wistfulness in her voice at the fleeting picture of Brede and the huts she had called home, and the lake she had so enjoyed—but the vision slipped elusively away and left only a vague feeling of regret.

'Don't fret yourself about me. There is nothing you can do to help in any event—Look, here comes your sister. I shall be here three days from now, probably. Perhaps I shall see you.' As Octavia approached, he inclined his head and walked away, smiling.

'He is handsome,' Octavia commented on the way home, 'for a gladiator. He has not so many scars as most. Does he spend all his time in the Forum?'

'I think he goes there for his—for the man who . . .' She floundered for the word.

'His trainer? He is one of Tibelius's "familia" I think. Flavius made enquiries about him. You know—' at Thea's blank look—'asked questions.'

Thea was conscious of a quickening of her blood but tried to keep the indignation from her voice. 'Why?'

Octavia shrugged her shoulders prettily and laughed a little. 'Who knows why Flavius does things? Perhaps he has an interest in you—as his foundling and as the cause of his return to the bosom of our family.'

Thea made a sound of disgust and said nothing, and their conversation moved to more general things.

At dinner that evening, she found herself seated opposite him, and although whenever she looked at him, his gaze was usually directed elsewhere, she had an uneasy feeling that he was, nevertheless, watching her, and the sensation sent icy shivers down her spine and set her stomach curdling. Only once or twice their eyes met and he acknowledged it with a mere flicker of amusement around his mouth.

'Will you walk with me in the garden?' he said when the meal was over and Thea, who had been listening intently to a discourse between Marcus and her father, turned with a tart refusal on her lips only to see that it was not she to whom he addressed his question, but Octavia. She turned quickly away again, blushing furiously at her stupid mistake. How foolish that she should assume he wished to walk in the garden with her!

Octavia did not hesitate to acquiesce and Thea wondered again just how deep Octavia's feelings were for him. Personally, she would prefer someone of a gentler nature—Gregor, for instance, who charmed rather than bruised her senses. Flavius and her sister seemed one of a kind and should deal well together. The thought, though, did not sit easily with her.

Thinking of Gregor reminded her of Octavia's disclosure earlier that Flavius had asked questions about him. No doubt he had spies everywhere—perhaps even Octavia would carry tales if she were fond enough of him—and she wondered if he would make trouble for Gregor if he discovered that she had spoken with him again, in defiance of orders. It would be a despicable thing to do, but she believed him capable of anything.

Later, when Flavius and Octavia had come back in and Thea was sitting by the open door, taking little more than a desultory part in the conversation, she found herself distracted by the fragrant scent of the night flowers. Excusing herself, she wandered out into the coolness of the evening. She was always fascinated by those strange, beautiful flowers that remained innocuously closed during the warmth of the daylight hours and opened only to the night's darkness and the silver moonlight.

She had thought only to stroll along the path to the farthest wall of the garden and then return, but as she paused by a pool that sparkled in the moonlight, a slight pressure on her arm made her start and spin round in fright. Flavius stood there. The moon was reflected in his eyes and he looked a little unearthly. 'Would you walk with me, Thea?'

She hesitated, but could find no reasonable excuse to avoid it. 'Octavia is happy to walk with you,' she said, irrelevantly.

'And you are not? Yet you blushed when you thought it was you I asked after dinner. I thought you were disappointed. Come.'

She silently cursed him. Was there nothing he missed? She turned and fell into step beside him, seeing no other alternative, but conscious of a tremor down her spine and a strange flutter beneath her ribs. She knew she was tense, every muscle seemed to have hardened and she was painfully aware of his hand on her arm, burning her flesh.

'Relax,' he said softly. 'I do not think I shall bite you. Not tonight anyway.' He paused and then smiled. 'Do you still believe we Romans eat children for breakfast? It seems to be a common belief among the barbarians and savages of our Empire.'

With a great effort, Thea restrained herself from slapping his face. 'Why do you make me angry every time we speak?' she demanded.

He looked at her and his lips twitched in mischief. 'Because I like making you angry. It amuses me.' He softened his voice. 'And when you are angry, your eyes become the colour of the water in Ostia harbour and you are very beautiful.'

He is laughing at me, she thought, forcing herself to keep her temper in check. If he was amused when she was angry, she would not give him the satisfaction of rising to his bait. He must find his entertainment elsewhere.

But in the darkest corner of the garden, he stopped, and a shiver that began deep inside her spread slowly through her slender body so that as he drew her into his arms, she was trembling violently. 'You cannot be cold,' he murmured, 'and you are surely not afraid with your family so close.'

She could find no words to answer. She was afraid, but not of him. It was her own body that frightened her, for she could not control the trembling, nor stop the churning of her stomach; and, worse, she could not pull away from him. His hand beneath her chin gently forced her head up; his eyes no longer reflected the moon but were fathomless pools of darkness.

His kiss was gentle but insistent. For a moment she stood rigid, his hands on her back held her against him, so close that she could feel every contour of his taut, muscular body. Then some other sensation stilled her trembling—a slow, dawning warmth that crept up through her, causing her loins and breasts and lips to tingle unbearably. She stirred in his arms, her lips moved beneath his in the beginning of response. Suddenly, as if she had released a tightly-wound cord in him, his kiss was no longer gentle, but hungry and searching and she felt the answering surge in her own body. She pressed herself against him without knowing what she was doing, every trembling muscle and prickling nerve tense with anticipation. His hands were gently exploring, gradually growing more demanding.

Suddenly she panicked and tore her mouth away, struggling. He made a sound, almost a groan, and released her, so abruptly that she almost fell. 'Go inside, Thea,' he said harshly. 'Go inside and go to bed.'

She turned and ran, but paused for a moment outside the door to allow the hotness in her face to subside and her breathing to slow, grateful that he showed no sign of following her. She plucked a night flower and, as she went inside, bowed her head over its sweetness to hide her confusion.

Pleading a headache, she went to her room in a turmoil. She could scarcely complain. Had she made any real attempt to avoid walking with him? Had she pulled away from him when he drew her into his arms? She sank onto the bed and began to unfasten her sandals with trembling fingers.

She wished she had more experience of such matters, of men. Brede, she knew, had lain with a man more than

MY DAUGHTER THELIA

once, and could twist them this way and that, at her whim. Octavia, too, had an air of knowledge about her, as if she would always know what a man's intentions were and when he was merely playing games. But she, Thea, had no such ability and had held herself aloof from the boys and men she had known, from choice at first and then through pride when the young men kept their distance without her bidding. Oh, she had been pecked by Brede's brothers, of course, chaste, fraternal kisses, but nothing to give her any experience of the arts and wiles of love-making and of men such as Flavius.

She took off her gown and for once left it lying carelessly on the floor while she unpinned her hair, took up a brush and began to draw it through the thick dark red locks that fell around her shoulders. Her cheeks burned at the thought of his kiss and his exploring hands and her body's betrayal in that moment of response.

When she went to bed, she lay with open eyes, unable to sleep. The more she tried to thrust away the memory of his caresses and the answering surge of her own blood, the more persistent it became and she spent a restless night.

Flavius seemed to find the time to come to the house on some pretext or other virtually every day during the following week and one day he gave her a present. It was a small gold cat, standing arrogant and beautiful, with arched back and erect tail, its eyes small, brilliant pieces of turquoise. She looked up at him with wide eyes. 'Why?'

He smiled faintly and shrugged. 'It reminded me of you. I thought you would like it.'

'I cannot accept it,' she said formally and held it out to him.

'But you must. Do not insult me, Thea, I wish you to have it.'

She bowed her head, and murmured: 'Thank you.'

He nodded briefly and left her, and she went at once to her room and buried it amongst her clothes, telling no-one and feeling acutely embarrassed.

That night, however, she was ready for bed, she took it out and held it in her hand admiring it. It was heavy for its size, but exquisitely and delicately made, all the beauty and arrogance of the cat captured.

'Thelia, I—' Octavia's voice at the door made her jump guiltily. 'Why, what is that?'

Reluctantly, she held it out for her sister to see. 'Flavius gave it to me.'

Octavia took it and turned it over in her hand. 'M'mm. It's pretty.' She gave it back and said goodnight, obviously forgetting what it was she had come for. Thea set the cat carefully on the table beside her bed and stared at it, wondering whether it had been to make Octavia jealous that Flavius had given it to her; he had spent a lot of time with Octavia these last few days when she, Thea, had avoided him because she did not trust herself alone with him.

She went to bed, and the cat's eyes shone in the darkness. She fell asleep, mesmerised by them.

The following day was the day Gregor had said he would be in the Forum and she found herself searching for some reason to go there herself. She broached the subject of an outing in the city with Marcus, but he was committed to spend the day studying.

Octavia, however, was happy to oblige. She had evidently spent some time luxuriating in the private baths the house boasted and was found in her room wrapped in towels and attended by several servants. 'Sit down in here and wait for me, then,' she said. 'I've little to do this afternoon. Perhaps we may meet some people there.'

Whilst the servants were intent on beautifying what Thea thought could surely not be improved, Octavia regarded her with a strange expression. 'Are you in love with Flavius, Thelia?' she asked suddenly.

She almost choked. 'No! Of course not!'

Octavia extended her hands to have scented oils massaged into them. 'It is only that you seem to take him so *seriously*. And the way you look at him sometimes when he is unaware of it—well, your face betrays your every feeling, dear sister, and it is so obvious.'

Thea's face was hotly crimson. 'But I do *not* love him,' she protested fiercely. 'I hate him.'

The elder girl sighed. 'You are such an innocent.' She waved the servants away and waited until they had gone before continuing, 'Since mother is no longer here, it is up to me to warn you,' she said, and went on slowly: 'You are not yet familiar with the ways of Rome. Flavius . . .' she paused delicately and picking up a long-handled mirror, surveyed her reflection.

'Flavius has a certain reputation,' she continued, 'not only with the women of high birth—of our own class—but also with the low-born women of the city. He went to Britain two years ago to escape from the demands they made upon him and the scandalous talk.' She paused and stood up, unwinding the long, soft towel. 'Of course, all that is forgotten now that he has found you and brought you home . . . Come, help me dress.' She picked up the garments that had been laid out on the bed and gave them to Thea, whose thoughts were in such confusion that she did not think that such a task was for servants and slaves.

'You are so obviously an innocent, dear Thelia,' she went on. 'A man like Flavius needs—diversions, challenges. Can you not see that he is merely amusing himself with you? His kisses and his caresses by moonlight in the garden set you trembling, no doubt, and his sweet words and flattery make you blush. And now he begins to give you gifts . . . but it merely amuses him. Sooner or later he will lure you to his bed with words of love and careless promises and then—' She broke off and shrugged her shoulders. 'Well, the next morning you are no longer shy and innocent, no longer amusing. You are just like all the others. Do you understand?'

She turned and looked at Thea with candid blue eyes and Thea nodded silently. She had understood enough anyway. She felt sick. Octavia was right, of course. Why, he had blatantly admitted that she amused him; he had flattered, caressed and kissed her and she—oh, what a fool!—had almost begun to believe . . . Well, she would not fall into his trap!

The turmoil of Thea's emotions evidently showed in her face. 'Do not look so shocked, Thelia,' Octavia said in a pained voice, 'I did not mean to upset you. Only to warn you not to fall in love with him. He will only hurt you.' Thea was silent, unable to voice her thoughts, and after a moment the elder girl added reflectively, 'Just think how the Gods favoured you on your voyage here by making you so ill. It was probably the best protection you could have had.'

Thea's memories of the voyage, however, were not so romantic. She had tried to block from her thoughts the knowledge that it was Flavius who had removed her sodden tunic, had applied cool, damp cloths to her burning body and replaced the covers over her when she had thrown them off in fever. She had thrust all this away, refused to allow that she remembered these things from the foggy delirium of those days. Unlike Octavia, she was inclined to believe that any protection she had from Flavius then was due to his need to deliver her safe and unharmed to Pontius than any charitable mood of the gods! Far more sensible from Flavius's point of view was to wait until he had safely used his charms to seduce her into becoming a willing victim! She did not disbelieve Octavia's words. She had hated Flavius from the beginning—surely she could not be blamed if she had momentarily been fooled by the sensations he had aroused in her?

Octavia's voice broke into her angry thoughts to announce that she was ready, and they went to the Forum where, once again, they left the litter and walked, Octavia chatting of irrelevant everyday things, and Thea concentrating all her thoughts on Gregor and anything that was not Flavius, at the back of her mind a simmering indignation.

She spotted the Briton sitting by a fountain and hung back from her sister hesitantly. 'There is Gregor,' she said shyly as Octavia turned to see what was wrong. 'Do you think I might—?'

Octavia seemed to hesitate, and then said, 'Oh, very well then. But you will have to catch me up. I shall wait by the Temple of Vesta and, for the love of Jupiter, don't be *seen* by anyone.'

Afterwards, Thea could not precisely recall what she and the gladiator had talked about but those few minutes went very quickly, and helped dispel the feeling of nausea Octavia's warning had created. When she rejoined her, Octavia looked sideways at her and said: 'Have you arranged to meet him again, Thelia? If you really wish it, I'm sure we could contrive something—'

'Oh, but Father would not wish—'

'He need not know of it. If we could think of somewhere less public for you to meet, there is no reason why he should come to hear of it. To meet a friend is surely not such a terrible thing.'

Thea said nothing immediately. Certainly the idea was appealing and she had to admit that she enjoyed talking to Gregor, however briefly—it was a light relief. She did not wish to upset her father and if they continued to walk unattended in so public a place as the Forum and meeting Gregor 'by accident', he could not help but hear of it sooner or later. So she agreed to the suggestion and confessed that he would be in the same place in three days time. 'Then we must ask him to meet you somewhere else,' Octavia said thoughtfully. 'I will think of a suitable place. And I know someone we can trust to deliver a message . . . .' Her voice trailed off in thought and she was quiet until some bright stall caught her attention.

That night, Thea considered sending the golden cat back to Flavius, but the thought of his reaction and of having to confront him and explain prevented her and she put it away in the bottom of a cupboard.

She spent much of her time with Marcus or with her father when his time permitted and with Cornelius, who was helping her to read. And she began to meet Gregor, with Octavia's help, in a little square seldom frequented by anyone they knew and usually at some hour unpopular for strolls in the city. There was always some reason to go out—Octavia was ingenious at it—visiting friends, or the baths, running some errand for a neighbour or relative . . . They seemed, to all intents and purposes, the closest of sisters and the best of friends.

The elder girl always slipped away and left them alone

for a few minutes. Gregor talked of his life in Britain before he became involved in a revolt against the Romans and was sent to Rome a prisoner for his trouble, and he told her of his plans once he found a ship and could escape. She listened, enthralled, and came away homesick, her imagination fired by the pictures he painted and her memory stirred up by his thirst for details of Boudicca's uprising and anything she could tell him about a Britain he had not seen for five years.

After one such meeting, she retired to her room and sat staring unseeingly at her little bird in its cage by the window, as it hopped from perch to bars twittering happily to itself. Her thoughts were far away, vaguely melancholy, as she tried to decide what her true feelings were about all that had happened to her over the past long months.

'Is this where you hide yourself?' She twisted round, startled, to find Flavius standing in the open doorway regarding her with lazy eyes. 'You seem to be avoiding me,' he said, pleasantly enough despite a grimness around his mouth.

Her own mouth was suddenly dry and her pulse seemed to be racing. 'I—have many things to do,' she murmured, quite disconcerted by his sudden appearance.

'Yes,' he agreed, 'such as meeting your gladiator friend. What fascination does he have for you, I wonder, that you go to such lengths to meet him?'

She stood up and glared at him angrily. 'How dare you watch me!' she cried. 'He is my friend and if I wish to speak with him—'

'You have other friends,' he said quietly.

'No,' she denied it vehemently. 'They are friends of

Octavia or Marcus or Father. Gryffgar—' She gave him his real name deliberately, '—is *my* friend. He speaks my language and speaks of things I understand and know. My home. He understands. You call me savage. Perhaps it is true. Perhaps it is too late to make me Roman again.' She lapsed suddenly into 'her' language, partly to express herself better and partly to annoy him. Why, after all, should she struggle for words? 'You should have left me where I belong for I am still Iceni in my heart and more like Gryffgar than you Romans! Gryffgar understands. Gryffgar—'

A stinging slap cut across her words and made her cry out. She stared at him in disbelief and then, in a blind fury, flew at him like a wild animal, trying to hit him and push him out of the door at the same time.

But Flavius was strong and coldly angry and merely held her at arms' length until the fury had spent itself. Then she drooped in his hold, her eyes downcast.

'I am to blame for your being here, Thea,' he said coldly. 'It is I you must hate, and hurt. Not your father. Do you realise what it would do to him to know you have secret meetings alone with a gladiator?'

She looked up at him briefly. Alone? Then she remembered that Octavia had always left them alone together, sometimes leaving her before they even reached the meeting place—out of consideration she had thought, but perhaps out of a sense of self-preservation. She could not blame her; it was enough that she had helped with the meetings. She lowered her gaze again. 'Father will not know.'

Flavius dug his fingers into her arms and gave her a single hard shake. '*I* know. And probably half Rome knows. And the only reason Pontius does not is because he is a well-loved man and no-one wishes to break the news that his daughter is making a fool of herself with an upstart gladiator!'

She pulled free of his grip. 'Why did you bring me here, to Rome? Why did you not leave me alone? Why?'

'Because this is where you belong! Do you truly believe you belonged there? Have you so quickly forgotten the huts that were no more than hovels? The cold, the loneliness of the moor, the endless struggle to find enough food simply to stay alive? The hardships, Thea, the long, hungry winter. Have you really such a short memory?' She felt tears sting her eyes and a lump rise in her throat. 'And do not think it has been easy for Pontius, suddenly to find himself with a daughter he thought dead, who seems totally foreign to him. Does his kindness mean nothing to you?'

'Kindness is not everything!' she snapped back perversely, hating him for thinking he had to remind her of such things.

Suddenly he caught her arms in a grip that made her cry out, and then he was shaking her mercilessly. She cried out in pain and fury, loosing a tirade of Iceni abuse as she struggled desperately to free herself.

Abruptly, he let her go and she staggered, red-faced and furious, refusing to let the tears into her eyes. He stared at her for a moment and then pulled her into his arms, kissing her harshly. There was no passion in it, it was a hard, brutal kiss and she, shaking with anger, was held in too rigid a grasp to fight him. Slowly his mouth softened and began to seduce her lips into parting beneath his insistent tongue, and her body gradually yielded in his arms. His hand moved down her back, caressing gently.

Then, suddenly and without warning, he pulled himself away, turned on his heel and walked out. She stared blankly after him, dazed at the abruptness of it, then sprang forward and banged the door shut behind him.

How she hated him! His arrogance was unbelievable. He thought he could do as he liked with her—charm and seduce her in order to get her into his bed one day, and insult her and treat her like a child the next! Shout at her and shake her one minute and then kiss and caress her a moment later. How dared he hit her? How dared he tell her who she may or may not see, or how she should feel about her father? Who did he think he was?

She paced the room angrily for a few minutes, too furious with him even to give way to the tears welling up in her eyes. She ought, of course, to tell her father what he had done—it was a wonder no-one had come running at her cries. She knew she would not and the rage ebbed slowly away, leaving her totally confused. She hated him for humiliating her so; she felt angry and insulted. And yet . . . her body yearned to feel his power, the strength of his arms, and the demands of his mouth . . .

The thought crept through her like a seeping dampness. Surely she could not love him—despite her belief that he was only using her as a diversion to ward off the boredom of his days? Despite the way he had treated her? Despite her determination not to make a fool of herself in that way? No. She shook her head. No, it was just that she had never met anyone like him before and he was having a strange effect on her. She had had the pride of the Iceni instilled into her blood and no mere Roman was going to destroy that!

Neither, she thought grimly, would she give up her meetings with Gregor merely because he told her to!

CHAPTER SIX

SHE went to meet Gregor the next time with an air of defiance, perversely hoping that someone would see her and report it to Flavius so that he would know that she had no intention of listening to him.

But as soon as she saw Gregor, she knew that something was wrong and her own preoccupation with Flavius was forgotten.

'It's nothing,' he said calmly. 'Merely a small problem.'

Thea, however, was not put off so easily and eventually, sitting on a wall and taking her hand, he said: 'There is to be a contest between me and Sejanus as part of an entertainment for Nero and some Alexandrians he has brought here to impress.' He paused and looked at her. 'Serji is one of the best, Thea, and a local too. He's always the favourite of the crowd and when he's in the ring they always demand his opponent's blood.' He shrugged his broad shoulders. 'This time, with Nero needing to show strength and power, they may well get it—a fight to the death. If I lose . . .'

He left the sentence unfinished and Thea looked at him in horror. 'You must escape!' she cried. 'Surely you can do something?'

'Escape?' he repeated sceptically and shook his head. 'No. I had great difficulty getting away today. Tibelius suspects I am up to something—perhaps I have been careless and too often seen with ship's masters and the like. I doubt he will let me out of his sight now until after the contest. He stands to win or lose a fortune on it, as well as his reputation and the pleasure of the Emperor. He'll not risk my disappearing. I was lucky today.'

'But—' Appalled, she floundered for something to say. 'Surely you must be his equal for them to have put you together to impress these Alexandrians? You have as much chance of winning.'

'Perhaps,' but there was little optimism in his voice.

'And they call us barbarians!' she cried. 'It is horrible. Is there nothing you can do?'

He shrugged his broad shoulders. 'I doubt it. I had hopes of a ship at last, but if I cannot get out to arrange things—'

'Let me help! Surely—'

'No, Thea!' The violence of his denial surprised her. 'You can do nothing and it is very dangerous. Promise me that you will not interfere in this.'

She nodded, 'Very well.' She was silent a moment then: 'When is to be?'

'In a week . . . but I must go now.' He stood up from the wall and gripped her hand more tightly. 'If you do not see me again, don't be too sorry. I would rather be dead than stay much longer a captive here.' He pulled her to him and gave her a brief kiss on her forehead. He looked at her for a long moment, then said quietly, 'Don't struggle against Rome, Thea, you belong here.'

He went quickly, his strange parting words lingering in the air where he had stood and she turned slowly away, feeling sick and hollow.

'Whatever is the matter?' Octavia demanded as they walked home. 'You look quite ill.'

'Gregor has to fight,' she said unsteadily. 'A man

named Sejanus. In a week, he said, for the Emperor and some visitors.'

'Oh, yes,' Octavia said cheerfully, 'Father said something about Nero putting up a show of strength for some people he has with him.'

'But Gregor does not think he will win. He will die, Octavia—'

'Nonsense. But of course you must see the fight. We shall both go!'

'Oh, no!'

'I am sure Father will be in Nero's party,' Octavia continued, ignoring Thea's dismay. 'Probably Flavius too, so we should be able to contrive something. The best seats, too! Especially as you found such favour with our dear Emperor.'

'But I could not, Octavia,' Thea protested, appalled at the thought of watching helplessly as Gregor was killed, and knowing that any reaction she showed would be keenly noted by her father and by Flavius—who no doubt would take great delight in Gregor's death. 'No, I cannot,' she repeated tremulously, tears in her eyes and her voice husky.

'You must. Perhaps your presence there will give him extra strength, something to fight for. Surely you owe him that much, Thelia?'

She was silent, wretched, wishing with every ounce of her strength that she had never set foot in Rome.

Octavia, however, took things into her own hands and very soon it was arranged. The two girls would go in Nero's party to the Public Games to be held in honour of the Emperor's guests. Thea spent hours agonising over it, yet knew that Octavia was right. She did owe it to Gregor, and she was vain enough to think that her presence really might help him.

So, in dread, she waited for the awful day in an absent-minded dream, to the exasperation of Cornelius and the concern of her father. She insisted that there was nothing amiss, but could concentrate on nothing, her thoughts filled with a sense of impending doom. If only there were some way of getting Gregor away—of finding a ship that would carry them both as far from Rome as possible, back to Britain, to familiarity and the strange comfort of a stark existence. Flavius had challenged her with its hardships, but at least the constant battle against hunger and cold did not allow time for the idle hours and idle thoughts that permitted such assaults on emotions and senses as Rome, and Flavius, made upon hers.

As the day approached she grew more tense and irritable, and one day spent several hours in the baths. Very few people in Rome itself—even the very wealthy—actually had private baths in their city houses, mainly of course because they were not nearly so spacious as their country villas and most preferred, in any event, the social event of a visit to the Public Baths. Pontius, however, had had part of the rear of his house made over to baths and Thea, her body aching with tension, retreated there on this particular evening in an effort to relax and rid herself of a raging headache.

She undressed quickly and wrapped a linen towel around her before going into a tiny room, sultry with warm air, where she settled down to let the warmth soothe her and empty her mind of all the nagging fears. She had almost drifted into sleep when the girl came to tell her that the 'solium' was ready and she moved into the adjoining room; the girl washed her hair and then left her to soak in a steaming hot bath which was perfumed with essence of cloves. She lay back and closed her eyes. There was a kind of sensual pleasure in the soft, gentle fragrance of the water as it lapped idly round her body and a delicious feeling of satisfaction in the knowledge that Brede would be horrified at her delight in the ritual bathing. She luxuriated in it, carefully thinking of nothing but how blissfully soothing it was.

She stayed too long in the steaming water and there were beads of perspiration on her face and red patches on her skin when she rose to immerse herself in the cold water bath next to it, the shock making her gasp. She repeated the hot-cold baths once more, emerging with a pleasant tingling sensation all over her, and moving into another tiny room, where the slave girl was waiting to rub her dry with soft towels and anoint her body with subtly fragrant oils. Finally, wrapped in another length of soft white linen, she sat on a couch and let the girl brush her heavy dark red hair until it was dry and gleaming.

Glowing and relaxed, her headache gone, she left the steamy room for the coolness of the corridor outside clad only in the towel, which barely covered her breasts and fell to just below her knees, hardly expecting to encounter anyone as she walked back to her room. As she reached the door, she was overwhelmed by a sudden wave of dizziness and closed her eyes for a moment, resting against the jamb of the door.

'Thea!' A memory sprang momentarily to life at the back of her mind. That same voice—full of alarm, half warning, half fearful; the rolling deck of a ship, the sting of spray, the safe, strong arms . . . She opened her eyes abruptly and Flavius released his grip on her arms. 'Are you all right?'

'Yes,' she said curtly. 'I stayed too long in the heat.' She began to move past him, but he barred her way and she was suddenly conscious of the scantiness of her attire. 'What do you want? You should not be here.'

'I was curious,' he said in a strange tone. 'Curious as to why you should want to go to see the Games. Do you really wish to see him die? He probably will, you know.' She looked up at him, recognising in his eyes a suppressed anger and involuntarily wishing he would not be angry with her now. 'I had expected you to shy away from such a spectacle,' he continued, disgust in his voice, 'but it seems you are just as thirsty for blood as any Roman woman. I thought you had a sensitivity they mostly lack, but it seems I was wrong. The savage in you will probably enjoy the sight!'

She looked away, her vision blurred by tears. Desperately she wished to protest that she would far rather not go, that Octavia had pushed her towards it, that to see Gregor hurt was the last thing she wanted and that she shuddered every time her thoughts even touched upon what might happen in the amphitheatre that day; but pride kept her silent and she tried to move past him again.

He stopped her, and put his hand beneath her chin, raising her head until she looked at him. His expression suddenly softened. 'Thea, I'm sorry. I did not mean to—' He suddenly bent his head and kissed her, entwining the fingers of one hand in her hair and holding her close against him with the other. She tensed at the firm touch of his fingers on her bare back, delicious shivers running down her spine, and let a little moan of helplessness escape her. Then, suddenly, there was Octavia's voice saying, 'Flavius needs diversions, challenges . . . he is merely amusing himself . . . he will lure you to his bed . . .'

She tore her mouth from his and thrust his arms away.

As she did so, he caught the towel and it slipped treacherously from her. With a cry of horror, she tried to snatch it back, but he held it behind him with a chuckle of amusement, his gaze sliding over her appreciatively, and then pulled her towards him. Draping the towel around her neck, he pinned her arms behind her with one hand and kissed her in a way that left her in no doubt of his thoughts. 'Thea, Thea,' he murmured huskily, his lips against her neck, crushing her hard against him and running his hand over her bare skin, that stung like fire at his touch. There was an intensity in his mouth as he sought hers again, an urgency as his hands explored . . .

'Please,' she said, almost in tears, 'Please, don't—'

He groaned, and a shudder ran through him. After a long moment, he drew the towel down over her, wrapping it tight around her as he raised his head. She kept her eyes downcast so that she would not have to look at him, and he turned her round, opened the door of her room and pushed her inside, closing the door behind her. She leaned back against it with closed eyes and hotly flaming cheeks, waiting for her heart to stop pounding, totally confused. She knew instinctively that he had been close, very close, to taking her there and then; and she also knew, horribly, that she would have had neither the strength nor the will to stop him.

She sprang away from the door, angry with herself, and began to get dressed. Later, when her embarrassment had subsided, she found herself angry with Flavius for another reason, recalling what he had said about her wish to attend the Games. Only a week ago he had told her that she belonged in Rome, implied that she should behave in a manner befitting the daughter of Pontius Aquila. Now it seemed he was unhappy that she *was* apparently behaving like Roman women and enjoying the sport and spectacle of the city. 'Curse him,' she thought crossly. 'What does he want of me? Why can I do nothing right?'

Strangely though, it was the cat he had given her to which she turned for help, bringing it from the cupboard where she had hidden it and setting it by her bed once more, praying that it might bestow some of its Roman luck on Gregor.

She dressed with particular care the day of the Games, but took little pleasure in the compliments she received from Nero and his guests. Only with a supreme effort did she manage to look and act as though she were enjoying herself and she was acutely conscious of the appraising glances Flavius gave her. When they finally took their seats, however, Octavia contrived to sit beside him and succeeded in diverting most of his attention. Judging by the laughter, he was not unhappy about it. Thea, sitting beside Marcus a little distance away, felt a momentary pang of something suspiciously like jealousy, and angrily thrust it away. Octavia was evidently well able to take care of herself and handle Flavius without embroiling herself in any of the dangers she had deemed it necessary to warn *her* about! Well, they probably deserved each other!

With that bitter-sweet thought, she turned away and studied her surroundings. The amphitheatre was full and buzzing with voices which fell quickly silent when Nero rose to give his speech; then there was a long sequence of contests—boxing, wrestling and gymnastic displays— then the gladiatorial contests.

The Games were essentially for display and Nero was in a wonderfully good humour so that most of the early, minor contests—if they had been closely and bravely

MY DAUGHTER THELIA

fought—resulted merely in the victor being showered with flowers and coins and deafened by the appreciative roar; and the defeated leaving the arena bleeding and wounded, totally disgraced.

However, there were one or two deaths, whetting the appetite of the crowd. Brought up as she had been, the sight of blood did not affect Thea unduly and she enjoyed the battle of wits and skill as much as anyone. The waste, however, when one was unnecessarily killed, she abhorred.

'Sejanus! Sejanus!' The roar thundered around the amphitheatre. Behind her, Thea heard the Emperor's laughter, and 'Now we shall see some sport my friends!' She turned away, so that he should not see the look of disgust on her face.

In another moment, the increased clamour of the crowd heralded the appearance of the two gladiators. Helmeted and armed with heavy swords, they were dressed in short leather tunics and had protective bindings on their wrists and forearms. Gregor looked taller, somehow, but the two men seemed to be of equal build and, indeed, the contest between them was a long struggle.

Thea sat through it, tense with apprehension, feeling as if Flavius's eyes were burning into her back. The sound of Octavia shouting encouragement to Sejanus rang coldly in her ears above the din of everyone else. How can she? she thought bitterly, and then excused her sister on the grounds that Sejanus was a Roman-born hero and Gregor only an ex-slave and a Briton.

Several times she flinched when the sword of Sejanus plunged towards Gregor. One such thrust drew a line of blood on his forearm. Another glancing blow, although inflicting a mere scratch, set him off balance and sent him spinning backward. Thea's heart was in her mouth as Sejanus lunged forward, but Gregor twisted away in time and the Roman's sword dug into the earth and cut a deep scar in the dust. As he stumbled to regain his balance, Gregor struck upwards, only to cut through the shoulder of Serji's tunic and draw a trickle of blood.

The animosity between the two men could almost be sensed, but so too could the mutual respect. Then, suddenly, the worst happened. Gregor's sword clashed violently against Sejanus's and spun out of his hand. The crowd seemed, as one, to gasp. Sejanus appeared almost to draw back, as if to allow Gregor to regain his weapon, such was the private respect they had for each other. But the commanding voice of Nero was heard above the crowd and as Gregor reached downwards, Serji leaped forward.

Thea bit her lips together and closed her eyes. There was a roar from the crowd and a long, shuddering sigh. She opened her eyes and felt a sadness wash over her at the sight of Gregor's inert form, the side of his tunic already soaked with blood. Sejanus was acknowledging the acclaim of the crowd, when suddenly Gregor stirred slightly. He was not dead! The collective voice of the people exclaimed the fact and Sejanus turned back. Thea drew a sharp breath. Surely not—? Nero rose and Sejanus, his sword poised over Gregor, turned to his Emperor for approval. Thea could not look round to see what Nero would do, but Sejanus, at his sign, suddenly threw aside his sword and extended a hand to Gregor and helped him struggle to his feet.

The crowd rose with cheers of approval and tumultuous applause as the two men made the necessary obeisance to Nero and Sejanus acknowledged the accolade of his supporters. Thea, too, was on her feet beside Marcus, smiling and clapping, but as they left the arena, Gregor looked barely conscious and was heavily supported by the two men who came out to help him, and she wondered if he would die anyway.

The rest of the proceedings were of little interest to her and she was relieved when it was all over. Pontius and Flavius were to go with Nero; Marcus announced that he was going to the Baths with Drusus, and Octavia and Thea were left to return home with several of the Emperor's guards as escort. As they left the amphitheatre Thea found Octavia beside her.

'If you wish to see Gregor,' she murmured, 'it might be possible.'

Thea looked at her quickly. 'But how—?'

'Silla!' Octavia summoned the servant. 'Silla will help you disguise yourself sufficiently—she knows where to go and what to do. I will deal with our escort. Do you wish to?'

Thea hesitated. It was a dangerous and foolish thing to do, and something about Octavia's over-willingness to help her to do things she ought not, rankled at the back of her mind. But Gregor had looked so badly hurt. 'Yes.'

Minutes later, she was following Silla through the streets around the amphitheatre. They stopped in an alley opposite a long low building which housed the gladiators; Silla bid her stay hidden and then disappeared, returning a few minutes later with a flask of wine. Under her direction, Thea looped her gown up into its belt and wrapped the girl's coarse cloak around her, pulling back her hair and concealing it beneath the hood. She exchanged her sandals for Silla's and took off all her jewellery. Finally, she picked up the flask and a few moments later stepped from the shadows, to all intents and purposes a common servant.

A fat, bald-headed man answered her timid knock, his breath reeking of wine. Almost Thea gave it up and ran, but she steadied her nerves. 'I have wine for the man Gregor,' she said as Silla had told her. 'Is he badly hurt?'

'He'll live.' The man's eyes raked her up and down knowingly. 'It's more than wine you have for him, eh?'

She lowered her eyes, blushing. 'May I see him?'

'Perhaps.' She put a few coins in his hand. He tossed them in the air and jerked his head in the direction of the passageway behind him. 'Third door.' Thankfully, she ducked her head and slid past him.

The door opened into a small, spartan room with rough walls and an uneven stone floor, its only furnishings a thin rug and a bed, on which lay Gregor, his face grey and his eyes closed. She pushed back her hood and knelt beside him, carefully setting down the jug of wine. 'Gregor?'

He opened his eyes and a flicker of surprise showed in them. 'You should not be here,' he said, his voice stronger than she had expected.

'I had to come. How bad is it?'

'Not as bad as it looks,' he said reassuringly. 'I'll be well enough in a week or two. You were there?'

'Yes. You look terrible.'

'Thank you!'

'Is there anything I can do? Anything you need?'

He shook his head. 'You must not stay, Thea. If anyone finds you here—recognises you—'

She shrugged. 'Don't worry. Would you like some of this wine?' He nodded and she helped him to lift his head and shoulders sufficiently to sip from the narrow-necked flask. His face was drawn with pain when he lay back, but he smiled at her. 'There *is* some good news . . . that ship. It sails for home in two weeks and I am promised passage.'

'Two weeks?' She could not hide her dismay. 'But you will not be strong enough for such a voyage, surely! If you are cursed with the same weather we had, it will kill you!'

He said nothing for a moment. Talking was an obvious effort. 'Do you begrudge me this chance, Thea?' he said, watching her. 'I have waited so long—'

She was instantly contrite. 'Oh no! I am very glad. But I fear for you.' There were lines of pain on his face, and he was breathing irregularly now. 'Don't talk any more. I do not—' She broke off at a sound in the passageway outside. 'I must go.' She pulled the hood back over her hair. 'I will try to see you again. Octavia seems to be able to arrange things like that. And if you need anything . . .'

He nodded and put out his hand. 'Goodbye, Thea.' She rose, then hesitated, looking at him. She might not see him again.

'Go, Thea,' he said gently. 'I'm grateful you came—but go now before you are discovered. We'll meet again before I leave.'

She nodded and then turned and went quickly, leaving the building unseen. Silla was waiting and, properly attired once more, they hurried back through the side streets to the house, a journey which seemed much farther on foot. She left Silla to go round to the rear while she herself went quickly inside.

'Thelia! Thelia, where have you been?'

Her heart turned over as she stood still and several lies

went through her mind. But her head went up as she faced her father's half anxious, half angry figure. Why lie? She was not ashamed that she had gone to see Gregor. He came towards her. 'We have been very worried about you, child. Octavia said only that you had something to do and refused to say any more.'

A movement behind him caught her eye as Flavius emerged into the passageway. She swallowed and drew a breath. 'I went to see the gladiator, Gregor.'

There was a long, awful silence. Pontius's face went purple. 'How dare you do such a thing when I expressly wished you to have nothing to do with such characters? Have you no shame? No pride? What in the name of the gods possessed you to do such a thing?' There was another heavy silence; Thea remained perfectly still. 'Answer me, Thelia! Why did you go there?'

'I—' She hesitated, a little afraid, then hurried on: 'He is my friend. I wished to see if he was badly hurt.'

'Your friend?' he repeated incredulously. 'How can such a man be your friend? Explain, if you please.'

She glanced at Flavius, wondering if he would tell Pontius about her meetings with Gregor; but he was regarding her with barely disguised amusement, evidently enjoying her discomfort. Well, she would not give him the satisfaction of watching her try to pacify her father with lies.

She raised her head and met his disapproving gaze steadily. 'I met him sometimes in the Forum, and then we arranged to meet in another place. It is good not to have to speak Latin, and to talk about home. And I like him.'

Pontius's face suffused with colour. 'You are not with the Iceni now, Thelia,' he said stiffly, 'you are in Rome and you will act accordingly. Go to your room immediately. We will speak of this later.'

With her lips tightly compressed and her head high, she moved swiftly past him, glanced fleetingly at Flavius as he moved out of her way, and went quickly to her room. She sat on the edge of her bed, put her head in her hands and wept. It was so unfair. She had not asked to be here, she had been brought, a virtual prisoner. It was so *stifling*. So many rules of behaviour, so much to learn and remember, so many restrictions; always someone wishing to know where she was and what she was doing. Oh, for one day in her coracle on the lake. One day alone, alone, alone. She might have been cold and hungry and afraid with the Iceni—all the things Flavius had thrown at her, but she had freedom at least. No-one questioned what she did or where she went. Even Brede's family, though they cared, let her go her own way most of the time. The homesickness stirred, an indefinable sadness. The poetry Gregor had seen in the hardships of his homeland, the pictures he had painted to colour her own memories . . .

'Perhaps he will take me with him.' She spoke aloud and then sat staring into nothingness, her tears drying, as the thought took root. She must see Gregor again—ask him, beg him to take her with him. Another thought, then—it would serve Flavius right if she ran away.

She ate little and said scarcely a word during dinner, answering Marcus's anxious questions with monosyllables—evidently no-one had told him what had occurred earlier. Once or twice she looked up and caught Flavius's speculative gaze upon her, but she was too preoccupied to do more than glare at him. She went to bed and fell asleep thinking about going home with Gregor, of the lake at sunset, and walking back across the heathered moor in her short tunic and sandals with a bundle of plump, gleaming fish. And of the expression on Flavius's face when he realised she had gone.

CHAPTER SEVEN

SHE slipped into Octavia's room early the following morning and found her still in bed.

'Thelia! For the love of Venus—what do you want at this hour?'

Thea sat on the end corner of the bed. 'I should like to see Gregor again.'

Octavia stared at her. 'Is that all you came to tell me?'

'I could not sleep. In two weeks he will leave and I should like to see him before he goes.'

Octavia seemed suddenly wide awake. 'He is leaving? Escaping? But how?'

'A ship.'

'But surely—is he not badly hurt?'

Thea frowned. 'He said it was not as bad as it seemed. But he looked so—so much in pain. He may need help.'

Octavia looked at her. 'You wish to try to help him escape from Tibelius? After that little scene with Father yesterday? Are you mad?'

'He is my friend—'

'Yes, yes,' she waved her quiet. 'You do not have to tell me. Save your protests for Father. Do you know the name of the ship? or when it sails?'

Thea shook her head. 'If I see Gregor again, I will ask him.'

Octavia's eyes narrowed. 'We'll go today then.' She

looked up and waved an imperious hand. 'Now go away, do.'

Thus dismissed, Thea wandered back to her room, and half the morning passed with a slowness she found intolerable until, finally, Octavia announced that she was ready.

As they reached the door on their way out, however, they were called back by Pontius, who demanded to know where they were going. 'To the Forum, Father,' Octavia replied, in a tone implying that she was surprised he asked. 'Do you need anything?'

'You may go, Octavia, but you will go in the litter and you will take one of the servants with you. I cannot allow you to go out unescorted. It really is not right. Since your poor mother died, you have had your own way far too much.'

'Very well, Father,' she murmured demurely and it passed through Thea's mind that Pontius had very little control over his eldest daughter, and that she would quite likely take no heed of him at all.

'But Thelia,' he continued, 'may not go. I am afraid that until I can be sure my wishes will be respected, I must confine you to the house. We shall review the matter in a week.'

'Oh, but I—' She began to protest and then stopped. To argue would only make matters more difficult. With commendable self-control, she lowered her gaze and said, 'Yes, Father.'

Octavia guided her back to her room and stood with her back against the closed door. 'You will have to stay, Thelia,' she said. 'It is no use looking like that. But I will take Silla with me and find out what I can.'

Thea stared resentfully after her when she was gone, angry at the indignity of being confined to the house like a naughty child. Later, when she was sitting by the partially open door staring uninterestedly at the garden outside, her thoughts solemn and far away, Marcus joined her with a pile of books in his arms, declaring that she could make good use of her time and astound Cornelius when he next came to the house. She smiled at him. 'You do not have to stay with me. I can amuse myself.'

He shrugged his shoulders. 'I want to. Besides,' he grinned, 'you do not seem to be having very much success amusing yourself.'

They spent perhaps an hour happily occupied, Thea trying to read, Marcus occasionally breaking off with a suddenly-remembered anecdote from his childhood, or an inquisitive question prompting her to tell him some story of her own. Her mood had lightened considerably until he thrust aside the books and leaned back in his chair. 'Are you happy here?' he asked her, his eyes, so like her own, regarding her thoughtfully.

'Yes,' she said automatically, and then caught his eye and looked away, flushing. 'I am not—unhappy.'

'Father does not mean to be harsh. He only wishes you to be happy and marry well. The trouble is, with our close connections to the Emperor, associating with the gladiator will only—'

'Marcus,' she interrupted, 'Gregor is a friend. I have lived all my life with such people and I find it very difficult to— to know that I may not even speak with him.' She met his gaze briefly and turned away, thrusting the long hair back from her face. 'Flavius should not have brought me here.'

'Don't be ridiculous! What else should he have done? And you surely would not rather be there than here. Besides—' he added in an attempt at lightness when she made no other comment, 'it brought him back. Octavia at least should be grateful to you for that since he went away only to avoid—' He broke off at a clamour outside and Flavius himself walked in.

'Marcus! What *are* you doing here, you idiot? We should have been at the palace half an hour ago! I've been waiting—'

Marcus leapt up in confusion. 'I completely forgot! I've been helping Thelia read. Wait here, I'll be ready in a moment.' He rushed out in a clatter. Flavius walked across to a chair and sank into it with an exasperated sigh, and Thea bowed her head over her book.

'You even bewitch your brother,' he said, mockery smiling in his voice.

She turned round slowly and looked at him. 'Perhaps he finds my company more pleasant than yours,' she said coolly.

He raised one eyebrow, faintly speculating. 'So you have learned to be cutting in our language, my dear Thea. Quite an achievement. And is reading becoming easier also?'

'No,' she said shortly, and turned back to her book. 'But I have to stay in the house for a week and there is nothing else to do.'

He was silent for a moment; then: 'Are you very unhappy here?'

Thea, suddenly, was sick of being asked that question. What did they expect her to say? 'Yes!' she snapped, swinging round to face him. 'Yes, I am unhappy. I hate Rome. I wish you had left me alone where I belong! I shall die if I stay here!'

He gave her a long, sharp look. 'Is it the gladiator? Are you in love with him?'

A surge of anger brought the colour flooding to her

cheeks. What right had he to ask such questions? Perversity stung her into answering forcibly: 'Yes! Yes, I am in love with him. Now are you content?' She stood up abruptly and walked quickly across to the window, standing with her back to him and looking out unseeingly.

'No, I am not content,' he said, and came to stand behind her, resting his hands on her shoulder. 'You are a fool if you think you love the gladiator. You are homesick, perhaps, and it is what he represents that you love. Come, look at me.' He turned her round to face him and lifted her chin so that she had no alternative. He held her gaze for a long moment and then said softly: 'You are a child, Thea, but you are blossoming into a beautiful woman. I could teach you so much, if only you would stop pretending to hate me, and stop being afraid of me. I would not hurt you, you know. You must learn to trust me.'

Deep inside her, Thea wanted to trust him, wanted to give in to those feelings that his every touch caused to surge up in her. She looked into his eyes, but could read nothing there. They seemed always to mesmerise her, to dissolve her own will into his, to make her knees tremble and her legs too weak to support her.

'Don't look at me like that,' he said strangely, and drew her towards him. A sound outside the door startled Thea out of her daze and she drew a sharp breath and pulled away from him, anxious not to be caught in such a position.

Marcus came back at that point and within a few moments they had bid her farewell and left her. She abandoned her books and sat on the couch, staring blankly at her hands. Flavius had her in turmoil. His very touch sent delicious shivers all over her—she was dangerously unable to control her emotions when he was close—yet at the same time his very presence seemed to arouse only anger and animosity in her. She had even allowed him to goad her into telling lies. She was not, of course, in love with Gregor, she merely wanted him to take her with him back to Britain, away from Rome and all things Roman! There things were safe, and she knew what she wanted and what was expected of her and where she stood with people.

She closed her eyes and her thoughts went round in confused circles until she drifted into sleep, to be awoken later by the return of Octavia, who had little news except that she had contrived to see Gregor briefly. Although he seemed well enough, he was suspicious of her and told her little. He had, however, expressed a desire to see Thelia before the end of the week and she had promised to try to arrange something.

The days dragged by interminably. Octavia might have curtailed her social outings a little to keep her sister company, but such a sacrifice evidently did not occur to her; indeed, she seemed to think that by relating to Thea all the gossip and colourful details of her every excursion, the younger girl's misery would be assuaged. Of course it was not; it was merely deepened. Marcus was busy with studies and his own social pursuits, which he contrived to follow rather more inconspicuously for Thea's benefit than did Octavia, and as Thea herself chose to keep out of her father's way whenever possible, she was a great deal abandoned to her own devices.

Flavius, however, spent an unprecedented amount of his time at the house. He, at least, seemed determined to help her pass her week of confinement as pleasantly as possible. She could only assume that he was prompted by feelings of guilt at her apparent unhappiness with

Rome. Or was he merely seizing the opportunity to try to seduce her? She began by attempting to avoid him, but he was very persistent and sought her out whenever she slipped away into a hidden corner, always with some titbit of gossip, or a box of sweetmeats from the Palace, or a book he thought she could read, or some trinket or toy to amuse her.

But it was not only her he came to see, of course! One morning as she was passing the door opening into the garden, she caught sight of him with Octavia beside the little oval pool. She could not hear them, but he had hold of Octavia's arm, and they were talking intently. Octavia turned and began to walk away, but he caught her and turned her towards him, obviously displeased. She shook her head and reached up and kissed him, and then drew away and came towards the house. Thea hurried quickly out of sight. Apparently Flavius was not having too easy a time with Octavia either!

One morning, when she was feeling particularly disgruntled, Flavius came upon her sitting curled on a couch, sulkily plucking all the petals from a flower, one by one, and dropping them with deliberate rebellion onto the floor. She looked up as he entered and felt a flush of irritation rise in her veins.

'That is a particularly childish occupation,' he remarked mildly.

'Why do you not go away?' she demanded. 'I wish to be left alone.'

He raised a sceptical eyebrow and perched on the end of the couch opposite her, 'Alone? Are you sure? What would you find to do to pass the time, I wonder? I'm sorry you dislike me so intensely but since your brother and sister seem to care very little how you spend the days and Pontius is far too occupied with more important matters to notice, I should have thought you would be grateful that I am giving up so much of my time for you.'

'It is not necessary. Please go away.'

He regarded her thoughtfully, then shook his head. 'I don't think I will.' He made the slightest of gestures towards the petals on the floor. 'Pick them up, Thea.'

She glanced down at the scattered pieces of flower and felt a momentary pang of shame at her childish destructiveness; but to have Flavius tell her to pick them up, as though she were a wilfully messy infant, rankled. 'I have all day,' she snapped. 'I do not wish to do it now.'

'You are in a very ill humour today, my little savage,' he said lightly, watching her from deceptively lazy eyes. 'Is there a particular reason for it, or are you merely out of temper?'

'How should I be?' she cried, and stood up abruptly, walking across to the window and staring out at the lovely day outside. She swung round and glared at him, her anger and frustration suddenly burst out in a flood of temper, the Latin forgotten in a stream of Iceni invective. 'How am I supposed to feel? Shut up like an animal in this stupid house—even the dogs and the slaves are not treated so! With the Iceni at least I could do as I wished, I was free to come and go as I pleased with no-one to treat me like a child. I cannot be closed up in here like this, I shall go mad! And merely because I talk to someone the all-important Pontius Aquila doesn't like! It's unbearable—'

Flavius, who by this time had risen from the couch, came unhurriedly towards her, took her face in his hands and kissed her. She was startled, yet not really surprised, and put her hands up to his chest to push him away, but somehow lost the power to do so. Her lips parted involuntarily and she stood allowing the leisurely, gentle kiss to send a slow warmth stealing through her veins. The anger ebbed away slowly and an indefinable yearning took its place. She began to feel she no longer had any control over her body or her emotions; that she was light as air and free as a bird. His hands moved over her shoulders, caressing her neck and her breasts and moving slowly down over her back. She trembled inwardly, feeling that her clothes were no protection at all, that his fingers burned her naked flesh. A heady recklessness swept up from her feet and swamped her reason; her whole body ached as she pressed herself against him, answering his kiss with every contour of her body.

Suddenly, he let her go and drew away. As she fell back from him she realised with a shock that in barely another moment she would have been begging him to take her, lost to his will for ever. A hot wave of shame coloured her face and she turned quickly away, appalled at herself. Yet somewhere at the back of her mind she wondered why he had stopped; was it not what he had wanted all along, her acquiescence?

The only sign in his voice that he had even noticed was a slight tautness. 'You should learn to be angry in Latin, my dear Thea,' he said, 'for your curses are otherwise wasted. Doubly so, when you look so dangerously beautiful.' She kept her back to him, rigid now and trembling violently. He opened the door and there was a moment's silence before he said softly, 'Be careful, little savage, that you do not tempt me too far. I am a mere mortal, after all.'

When she swung round, a retort on her lips, he was gone, and she wondered if she had quite understood him correctly. Was he daring to suggest that she had deliberately provoked him into kissing her? If so, he had a wondrous imagination! But what had she been thinking of to allow him to kiss her, to touch her in that way? After all the vows and resolutions she had made not to let it happen again! Octavia had been right to give her such warnings about him, but it was rather about herself she should have been warned. She *must* be more guarded. Why, if he had not pulled away when he had—It did not bear thinking of. Flavius was very dangerous and very clever and she would have to be so careful. If he thought her easy prey, but for a little concentrated effort on his part, it was her own fault. Whatever had happened to her pride?

With a dark, unhappy look in her dark blue eyes, she returned to the couch and slowly began to pick up the scattered petals. The problem, she reluctantly admitted to herself, was that he held a strange fascination for her. The very fact that he held danger, that Octavia had warned her of his reputation, of his mercenary dealings with women and uncaring, calculating attitude, perversely attracted her. And he aroused in her such a yearning, such tremblings . . . Certainly she tried to avoid him, but when he sought her out, was there not an alluring quality about him she found desperately hard to resist? It was like being close to a fire, knowing it would burn her but nevertheless being powerless to deny the beckoning tongues of flame that licked out to draw her towards its blazing heart. His kisses, undeniably, were like fire. He set her body tingling and her veins coursing with excitement. A delicious mixture of fear and desire . . .

She stood up abruptly, crushing the petals in her fist and shutting out such thoughts. It was inconceivable that she could actually enjoy such encounters with a man as arrogant and conceited as Flavius! It was Pontius's fault for confining her to the house and thus allowing her to fall prey to such fanciful notions! She would just have to keep a far greater control over her emotions and senses and find some positive occupation to keep her idle mind from wandering into daydreams about the unbearable man! She must never let him come so close again.

As it happened, other events temporarily took her mind off the state of her feelings towards him. Octavia went out on several mysterious errands during the closing days of that interminable week, about which she was particularly reticent. Then, one afternoon, happening to glance out of a window at the side of the house as she passed, Thea's attention was caught by the sight of her sister talking earnestly with an unsavoury character in the shadows of the garden wall. She drew to one side, careful that she could not be observed, and as she watched, Octavia glanced round, then dropped something into the man's hand. It appeared to be a rather heavy purse and it was quickly secreted amongst the folds of his drab, ill-fitting tunic.

Thea spent some time wondering whether to ask her sister about this suspicious meeting, but Octavia had not seemed very approachable lately and she was reluctant to challenge her. In the end, she contented herself with a casual question as to whether she had arranged about seeing Gregor.

Octavia was annoyingly evasive, saying merely that something was in hand and she hoped to have an answer by tomorrow. 'Really, Thelia,' she went on, 'you must not ask too many questions. I have no intention of telling you anything until a meeting is actually arranged, for you are so excitable you are bound to give everything away. And if Father finds out about this, all the time and money I have spent on your behalf will be totally wasted! Now, please, don't pester me!'

Annoyed at the implication that she was indiscreet, Thea nevertheless had to be content. She was not at all satisfied for it seemed to her a rather heavy purse Octavia had parted with if it were merely to arrange for her to see Gregor—and very unwise to give it away without any guarantee that a meeting would take place. However, she knew little of the ways of Rome and her sister's tone had been sufficient to deter her from probing any further.

The following day was the day Pontius had promised to 'review' her confinement to the house. Having presented a duly contrite face to him throughout the week and made him feel positively guilty at his severity with her, she was quite forgiven and allowed once more beyond the bounds of the house, albeit with a promise extracted from her that she would have no further encounters with the gladiator. This promise Thea gave with the merest pang of conucience, absolving herself with the merest pang of conscience, absolving herself gone and, perhaps, she with him. She had a momentary, sunset-tinted vision of herself standing on a ship's deck with Gregor, sailing at last from an alien and hostile land to the comfort and familiarity of home.

Octavia slipped into her room before dinner that evening. 'Gregor will be coming to the side gate at eleven o'clock tonight. I have bribed Lucius to leave the gate unlocked so you will be able to get out.'

'Oh, Octavia, thank you. I do not know how you—'

'It's better you do not,' Octavia interrupted. 'Do not thank me yet for he may not be able to get here. He is still not strong and a friend will aid him across the city. But it was an impossibility to arrange any other way without a great risk of Father finding out. So—' and this in a severe warning tone— 'be careful that you are not seen and do not linger. Lucius will lock the gates again half an hour later.'

Thea was shaking with the fear of discovery as she crept silently out of the house that night. Everyone but Pontius had retired to bed early and the faint glimmer of lamplight on the mosaic beneath his study door showed that he was still working as she stole past.

There was a fine mist of rain in the air, little more than a dampness, and she huddled her cloak around her and trod noiselessly through the garden. The side gates were shrouded in dark shadows as she eased them open and slid out into the darkness of the narrow street. Two men stood beside an ass which was tethered to a post a little way down and one of them detached himself and came slowly towards her. Although she could not clearly see his face, she could tell by his laboured breathing that the journey through the city had taken its toll of Gregor's strength.

'You should not have come,' she whispered. 'This damp—'

'It's nothing,' he said, taking her hand. 'I had to come. Everything is arranged, the ship sails in little over a week.'

She wanted to ask him to take her with him, but he looked troubled about something and somehow she could not bring herself to frame the words. Doubts, suddenly, came crowding in. 'How are you now,' she asked instead. 'Will you be all right for such a voyage? I am worried about you—'

'Don't be, then, because it takes more than this scratch to kill me. The thought of going home at last will give me strength enough.' They were silent a moment, only a slight breeze stirring in the leaves above them.

'Thea,' he began slowly, and hesitated. Then: 'If you really cannot stomach Rome—if you are really unhappy here, I can take you with me. It will be very dangerous for you, but . . .'

She looked away and bit her lip, a sinking feeling in her stomach. He was obviously reluctant. He did not really want to take her, and of course it was not fair of her to ask him. Her presence would hinder him, make everything more difficult, add dangers. She shivered in the dampness of the night air and remembered, reluctantly, bitter nights with scanty shelter and few warm clothes and food enough only by a miracle—Flavius's voice asking her how she could so easily forget. She tried to push away the picture and the undeniable truth of what Flavius had said, but this time they would not go away.

She felt torn in two, the conviction of the past week or so that she could not bear to stay in Rome any longer suddenly falling apart, shaken by Gregor's reluctance and her own doubts now the decision had to be made. Was being answerable for her actions so terrible a price to pay for the safety and luxury she had inevitably begun to take so much for granted—the plentiful exotic food, the permanent warmth and comfort, the baths, the elegant clothes, the flattering attention, servants and slaves to do her bidding; a family? Would she truly be able to settle into the harsher, more rigorous life of Britain? Her presence with Gregor would undoubtedly add incalculable risks to his own safe escape and if it failed she shuddered at the thought of what might happen to him if he were caught.

'No, Gregor,' she said suddenly, and steeled herself to convince him. 'No, I cannot. It has taken a long time but I am beginning to settle in Rome and it—it would not be easy to go back now. I know that. And it would be a terrible cruelty to Father.'

'Are you certain? You may not have another chance.'

She shook her head. 'No. I am very grateful, for I know well enough what risks you would have to take for me, but you must go alone.'

He nodded briefly and squeezed her arm. Even in the darkness she sensed his relief. 'It's not that I do not want to take you,' he said, 'but it would be a mistake, Thea. You would never be happy back there, not after all this. You do not know how you have changed since I first met you, how much more Roman you become with every week. Latin words even slip into your speech and you do not realise it. This is your home, Thea, where you belong, and you should stay.'

She nodded, and after a moment he drew a breath and said slowly, 'Be careful of Octavia, Thea. She offered me a great deal of money if I would take you with me and threatened to make sure Tibelius knew all about my plan to escape if I did not.'

'Octavia?' Thea was incredulous. 'But—'

He put his fingers to her lips to silence her and went on, choosing his words with care, 'Either she holds your happiness very dear or else she is a very dangerous woman. Don't trust her, Thea. You trust people far too easily.'

'And you are suspicious of everyone!' she retorted. 'Octavia has been a good friend to me. She's a little selfish, perhaps, but I am sure if she threatened you it was merely to ensure my happiness. She probably believes I am in love with you and that I'm terribly unhappy in Rome. She only wants to help me, really. Don't worry about her. When she realises the truth of it, she will not make any trouble for you.'

'Gregor!' His friend across the street hissed a warning. 'We must get back.'

He raised an arm in acknowledgement and turned back to Thea. 'I hope you are right about her. Promise me you will be careful.'

Time was getting short. It was raining harder and they were both shivering. Every moment they stood there was dangerous for him. 'Yes, I promise. Go now and be careful. I'll pray to all the gods to deliver you safe to Britain.' She reached up and kissed him, then slipped quickly back inside the gate so that he would not linger.

CHAPTER EIGHT

IN THE morning, she felt the loss acutely. She had taken Gregor's presence across the city so much for granted, drawn such comfort from the thought of having a friend, a refuge should she need it. Now he was gone, and she was conscious of a momentary, acute, sense of loneliness. She shook herself free of it. It really was too late to go back, she would simply have to face up to her new life and make the best of it.

Gregor's warning about Octavia, however, was not so easily dismissed. Surely, if Octavia had believed she was unhappy enough to think seriously about running away, she would have tackled her about it, especially if she was so concerned about her well being. Thea could not believe she had given her sister cause to think that she was desperately in love with Gregor. Of course, she had declared it forcibly in a moment of temper to Flavius, who also, because of her earlier outbursts, could be in little doubt of her unhappiness. Probably he had told Octavia; they seemed very close after all. She would not allow herself to think too badly of Octavia, and was convinced that she had only been acting in her best interests. Gregor had probably misunderstood that air of superiority she always wore when dealing with 'lesser' creatures. Nevertheless she could not help feeling aggrieved that she had not even been consulted about something that so directly concerned her, and more than a little angry that Octavia would actually bribe and threaten Gregor. For all her beauty and charm, her sister evidently had a great deal to learn about what money and power could *not* achieve.

At the earliest opportunity she assured Octavia that despite her unnecessarily strong efforts on her behalf, she would not be going with Gregor and did not wish to return to Britain.

'Well, you ungrateful brat!' Octavia exclaimed. 'I was merely doing what I thought you wanted. You have scarcely seemed to be enjoying yourself here and you *have* been making a fool of yourself over him!'

Thea's head went up in a proud tilt. 'You were mistaken, Octavia. And as Gregor would gladly have taken me had I wished to go with him I hope you will not make trouble for him with Tibelius. It is not your concern, after all.'

Octavia tossed her head haughtily. 'Well, of course not, you stupid child!' She whirled around, walking away with an offended air and giving every impression of completely washing her hands of her young sister's affairs.

Thea immediately felt annoyed with herself. The last thing she wanted was to make an enemy of Octavia. But really she could not go on being allowed to assume that because she had gone out of her way to be kind and helpful, she then had a right as a matter of course to interfere in any way she wished. If she was upset, Thea, decided, it could not be helped.

She felt in desperate need of diversion, something to take her mind away from both Gregor and Octavia and, indeed, from speculative thoughts of the future. So she went in search of Marcus, but as she passed the room where her father was working raised voices, through the partly open door, made her pause.

'But she is such a little fool!' Octavia was saying indignantly, 'Why everyone is making such a ridiculous fuss over her, I cannot imagine!'

'Octavia, really! The poor child has suffered so much. There are years to make up—'

'And she is making the most of it! She has you all running round after her, making allowances and worrying every moment that she is unhappy, lavishing her with attention! Why, she has bewitched you all! Everyone showers her with presents, everyone from Nero downwards. Even Flavius! She was better left where she was.'

There was a loud thump, as if Pontius had brought his fist down hard on his desk. 'Enough!' Thea caught her breath. Never had she heard him so angry. His voice shook with emotion. 'She is your sister, Octavia, and she has long been deprived of the things you take so easily for granted. I asked your opinion of this trinket because you have seemed so close these past few weeks. It pleased me to see you so. But this—!'

There was a moment's silence, then Pontius continued in a calmer voice: 'I know you had hopes of marrying Flavius yourself before he went to Britain, but he is not for you. I have a great desire to see Thelia and Flavius wed, Octavia—' a strange, strangled sound from Octavia interrupted him, but he continued: 'be warned, daughter, it is my dearest wish that this should happen and you must get used to it. Flavius is not for you and I will not countenance you making any trouble with your unwarranted jealousy.'

Thea heard no more. Choked by tears of anger and disbelief, her hands over her ears to shut out the betraying voices, she turned and fled. But her headlong flight sent her crashing into the arms of Flavius who was nearly knocked sideways as she careered into him. 'Ye gods, be careful!' he exclaimed, instinctively steadying her. 'What on earth has happened?'

She struggled in his arms, tears streaming down her face. 'Let me go! It is your fault Octavia hates me. It is *all* your fault and I hope you are well pleased with the trouble you have caused!'

He caught her shoulders and held her still, until she looked up at him. 'Now what are you talking about?' But Thea had suddenly lost her power to speak and felt herself tremble. Pontius wanted her to marry him! The enormity of it overwhelmed her. A door opened behind them and momentarily distracted him, and as his grip on her slackened slightly, she pulled free and slid past him, rushing towards the door into the garden.

On a stone bench in a shadowy corner, she put her head in her hands. Flavius did not know what he had done, bringing her here and causing so much trouble. She could scarcely believe what she had heard Octavia say. How could she be so friendly and pleasant one day and so horribly jealous the next? The shock of hearing such venomous words from the lips of someone she had begun to trust and envy had shaken Thea badly, but the thought passed fleetingly through her mind that it was her own fault for upsetting Octavia earlier. The outburst she had overheard had been little more than the tantrum of a very spoiled young woman who did not like her actions challenged by an upstart little sister she had thought to dominate. If that was the way of it, Thea thought, with some of her composure returning, then it was indeed her own fault. She could only admit that she had done her utmost to please Octavia and had been all too anxious to make a friend of her. She had accepted her help in meeting Gregor gratefully and without question, and without realising how much of a hold over her it gave the elder girl.

Her father's words had made it clear that Octavia and Flavius were to have been married before he went to Britain. And now it seemed that he was nursing a bizarre desire for *her* to marry Flavius. Of course, he was doomed to disappointment—Flavius would never agree to such an absurd idea. Thea herself could only hope that her father did not broach the subject with her first—it was an intolerable position and whichever way she turned she would surely upset someone.

If she told him she could not countenance marriage to Flavius, he would be hurt and disappointed; yet if she allowed him to believe she was willing, and relied upon Flavius to put an end to the plan, Octavia's resentment would know no bounds. How could she ever hope to be happy here when everything was always so complicated and confusing, so full of problems and emotional whirlpools?

The sound of footsteps roused her. She knew it was Flavius even before she looked up to see him coming, grim-faced, towards her. 'I have seen Octavia,' he said, looking down at her. 'It seems she said some unforgivable things.'

'Yes,' Thea murmured, wondering how he had contrived to make her admit to her spite.

'You must understand that she has been adored and spoiled by Pontius for many years, ever since you were given up for lost. Marcus is his son and a son will always be undisputedly special, not to be ruined by softness or over-indulged, but guided and moulded and disciplined. A man's daughter, however . . .' He shrugged a broad shoulder. 'I am afraid Pontius has pampered Octavia beyond redemption and—'

'I am not a child, Flavius,' Thea said slowly. 'I understand that Octavia is jealous. I also understand that it is because of your insistence in bringing me here! And now that Father has told her he wishes us to marry—!'

'Does he?' The curt demand cut across her words, and she looked up to meet his dark, penetrating gaze. So Octavia had not told him that! 'Yes,' she said. 'It is ridiculous, of course, and quite impossible.' Her light, careless tone belied the sudden flutterings in her stomach. If only he would not look at her like that.

His face, without actually changing expression, seemed to set into a rigid, impenetrable mask, and then, in another moment, relaxed. 'Do not fret, child,' he said with a whimsical smile, 'I will inform your father, in the nicest possible way of course, that his plan is quite obviously absurd.'

He is laughing at me, she thought, and was quite surprised at the pang of hurt she felt. But she kept her voice steady. 'Yes that would be best.' She got to her feet, dismissively changing the subject. 'Do you know where Marcus is?'

The following evening, Marcus came back from visiting friends with the news that the Emperor had announced a special chariot race to take place in seven days' time. Flavius had declared his intention of taking part and had gone immediately to his villa in the country to prepare for it. Marcus was in a high state of excitement and when Thea demanded to know what was so particular about *this* race he explained:

'It's a whim of our illustrious Emperor. A chariot race for the sons of Rome's richest and most prestigious citizens!' At her puzzled expression, he elaborated: 'Charioteering is *not* a respectable occupation for the wealthy, although one or two sometimes manage it, much to the horror of the stiff-necked! Flavius used to compete frequently, just to upset everyone. It upset Father most of all, I think, although Flavius always maintained he was secretly pleased if he won. Anyway, Nero definitely enjoys chariot races—has even competed himself occasionally, although of course no-one is shocked and the others have to let him win. And now he has decided to hold these races especially for all the "sons of the wealthy". No professional charioteers allowed.'

'Don't you wish to be in it?' she queried.

'Of course! But Father won't hear of it. Anyway,' he went on, 'Flavius is one of the favourites now. Everyone is in a stew over it—a week's notice does not give anyone much time to prepare, and Flavius has not driven a chariot in a race like this for years.'

Marcus's excitement and enthusiasm about the race was infectious and it helped dispel a little of the tense atmosphere generated by Octavia's hostility. Thea, for her part, was content to let her sulk, having much else to cloud her thoughts. Marcus was a willing enough companion with whom to while away the hours talking about chariots and races and Flavius's chances of winning.

Octavia's outburst evidently had little effect on Pontius, for he produced the 'trinket' one evening when the two of them were alone and she gasped at the sight of it. A gold filigree necklet set with ivory and coral. No wonder Octavia had been jealous for surely she did not own anything so fine! It was on the tip of her tongue to refuse the gift, but she knew that would only be an attempt to pacify Octavia and such a gesture would probably be wasted on the elder girl. And it was such a beautiful necklace. Anyway, one look at her father's face banished the thought—he would be so hurt. So she allowed the delight she felt to show in her face and thanked him shyly.

He put it on for her and fastened it, and then stood her at arm's length and looked at her, his eyes moist. 'Thelia, Thelia . . . so many years . . .' Thea felt an uncomfortable lump in her own throat and impulsively hugged him. 'I am here now, Father. Those years are nothing.' He patted her back and nodded, then set her from him, turning quickly away. Sensing his emotion and fearing that if she stayed longer he might bring up the subject of Flavius, she excused herself rather hurriedly and bid him goodnight.

Thoughts of marriage to Flavius plagued her continually. Surely it could not actually happen? Yet, somehow, at the back of her mind was the thought still that Romans could do anything, and that somehow Pontius would be able to make it happen, despite any views Flavius might hold on the subject. And she could not believe anything of him other than that if he married anyone it would be Octavia, and his interest in 'the little savage' was purely as an amusement—to play games with her and stun her senses and confuse her wits and finally lure her into willing submission and into his bed.

Very probably he had made the decision to enter the race and disappeared out of Rome purely to avoid any discussions about the marriage Pontius dreamed of. Her own feelings betrayed her, for although she often professed to hate him, hate was a stronger emotion than a girl such as Thea could maintain falsely for very long and her hatred for Flavius had subsided into something nearer defensive aggression. He was infuriating; he mocked her, treated her like a child, always seemed so easily to have her at a disadvantage. And the knowledge that he had seen her sick, wretched, naked and at her very worst sent waves of embarrassment over her every time she thought of it.

Yet the prospect of marriage to him did not appal her as it should have done! His powers to arouse her body to a trembling beyond her control, and set the blood rushing through her veins, she knew well enough. How easily she had responded when he had taken her in his arms that last time! At the back of her mind, did she not sometimes find herself imagining what it would be like to share his bed? To admit, even to herself, that she had such thoughts set her cheeks burning with shame. But there were other things, qualities that she had, however reluctantly, to admire. There was a strength about him, a confidence and a sureness—something that gave Thea the instinctive impression that any woman Flavius called wife—despite an inevitable battle of wills, for she could not imagine him wed to a meek and doe-eyed girl— would stand protected by him against all the evils of the world. Not of course that she would need protecting if that woman were Octavia!

She lived in dread of Pontius approaching her about his plans, mostly because she found herself acknowledging that she was not at all sure how she would answer, except that she could not conceive of marriage to someone who so clearly did not love her. But Pontius did not mention it and she wondered whether Flavius had indeed found time before departing to his villa to dissuade her father from such a course. Pontius, indeed, acted as if nothing was further from his thoughts. He seemed totally oblivious both to Thea's preoccupation and Octavia's blatant coolness towards her younger sister.

Thea found herself looking forward with as much anticipation as Marcus to the approaching chariot race. She was forced to acknowledge that despite the confusion of emotions his presence aroused in her, the house had seemed to her quieter, and the days strangely longer, without Flavius's visits, now that almost a week had passed since that last encounter. She did not try to convince herself that it was merely the prospect of the race which quickened her pulse. She was conscious of an inner tremor at the thought of him, an almost delicious tension as she recalled how magnificent he had looked at the reins of the chariot that had sped her away from the moors and the Iceni.

They had been invited to attend the Race as guests of Nero and to travel to the Circus as part of his entourage, an honour which Octavia clearly thought had more to do with the favour Thelia had found with their distinguished Emperor than any regard he had for their father.

The Circus was packed to capacity, a colourful sea of people in holiday mood. Most of the competitors had adopted a colour of one of the regular chariot teams—red, white, blue and green, and their families and friends had come armed with the appropriate ribbons and banners. Under her cloak, Thea wore a white gown trimmed with blue. She had blue silk threads in her hair, and carried a small gold stick on which were attached long blue ribbons.

The main race was to be preceded by twelve shorter races, each between two chariots only, the result of the fierce rivalry and private challenges between the competitors when the race was first announced. This had seemed the best way of solving the problem and the

Emperor had decreed that only the winners of these would go on to compete in the main event, for which there was a prize of sixty thousand sesterces.

First there was the traditional opening procession that seemed to Thea to go on for an age, an endless parade of dignitaries in ceremonial robes, officials bearing offerings to the gods and competitors in the beribboned chariots pulled sedately by immaculately-groomed horses.

The chariots for the short races were drawn only by two horses, since many of the drivers were complete novices despite their own inflated opinions of themselves. They were to complete only three laps of the long oval Circus, instead of the normal seven. The first two competitors eased their chariots into position, one on either side of the gate on which sat the starter. He dropped a white napkin, the crowd cheered, the horses bucked—and the race had begun.

The chariots charged down the length of the oval, turned round the sharp curve at the end of the central 'spina' and raced up the other side, sending up plumes of dust and skidding dangerously at the curves. At the end of the third lap, the winner was the charioteer who drove past the starter first, provided no cheating or foul driving had been seen. Not, of course, that it was possible to see such practices anyway at the speed at which the chariots hurtled round and through the cloud of dust they threw up.

Thea watched with growing excitement as these races progressed. She expected at the start of each one to see Flavius appear, but she had an agonisingly long wait for he was almost the last of the twelve pairs of competitors. She drew a breath and felt her blood race at the sight of him, tall and erect in his blue tunic with the long-bladed charioteer's knife thrust into his belt, and a whip in his hand, his cloak billowing gently behind him in the breeze. The grey horses strained at the reins, blue streamers flying from their harness, and she felt a swell of pride in her breast, almost as if he were hers to be proud of. But she justified the feeling on the grounds that he was almost one of the family and their only representative in the race.

The napkin dropped, and the horses leapt into motion. It was a close race and Thea sat on the edge of her seat, unable to keep still and oblivious to everyone else as the two chariots sped round vying for the lead. She waved her golden stick madly and joined her voice to that of Marcus beside her in cheering him on. In the last half-lap he drew ahead and, in the end, crossed the line easily the winner. Thea sat back with a gurgle of laughter, totally caught up in the festive atmosphere enveloping the Circus and the thousands of people packed into it.

After the last of the challenge races, which had taken in all over two hours to complete, there was a welcome lull in the proceedings while the chariots were hitched to four-horse teams. For those fortunate enough to be in Nero's party, slaves served wine and specially prepared titbits of meats, breads and sweet delicacies which melted in the mouth.

A buzz from the restless crowd drew Thea's attention from these delights back to the scene in front of her where the chariots were being led into their starting positions, six either side of the starter's gate and following the curve so that, supposedly, none had an unfair advantage, although Marcus, when he saw where Flavius was drawn, remarked, 'Pity he could not have been nearer the centre.'

'Why?' she asked, watching intently as Flavius stepped up into the gleaming chariot.

Marcus shrugged. 'They say the middle positions are the best—the inside ones can be dangerous if one of the chariots outside you takes the turns too sharply, and the outside ones can be a disadvantage because of the risk of being overtaken on the inside and losing speed in going too wide into the turns.' Thea nodded and turned her eyes back to the line of chariots. Flavius had two others on his inside. Immediately on his outside was the red-clad Linnius, whom Marcus informed her was Flavius's main rival, the other danger being Aulus, who was on the far side of the starter. The rest of the competitors Marcus dismissed out of hand as merely making up the numbers. 'He shouldn't have too much trouble,' he went on with undisguised admiration. 'His lead horse is the best animal out there. The best horses are always put at the front of the team on the left. See, the dark grey with the white mane.'

A rope was held across the front of the chariots to restrain them and there was a torturous wait while the starter got ready and the horses were quietened. An expectant hush fell on the crowd. Thea's every muscle was tense and she scarcely knew whether to watch Flavius or the starter's napkin, which was held tantalisingly aloft. Then, suddenly, there was a flutter of white, the rope dropped, the crowd exploded and the chariots jerked forward—almost, for an instant, as if taken by surprise. Then they were roaring past at an alarming pace and Thea was jumping up and down in frantic excitement.

There were seven laps to complete. By the end of the first, one chariot had skidded badly at the first turn and crashed into a corner, fortunately without injury to either driver or horses but with irreparable damage to the chariot, and the driver of another had completely lost control and his team careered wildly all over the track, almost causing disaster and eventually having to be caught by officials and pulled in complete disarray out of the path of the other teams.

'Come on! Come on!' Thea squealed, brandishing her blue ribbons, her voice all but drowned among the shouts and cheers of the people around her.

A fair-haired charioteer in green led, Flavius and Linnius were neck and neck behind him and Aulus was lost in a group of four chariots chasing them as they charged past the Emperor's canopy for the third time. Her heart leaped into her mouth and she held her breath in delicious fear at every turn as the chariots plunged recklessly into the sharp curves, skidded horribly, came perilously close to each other and finally regained control to race up the other side again.

Aulus was the unfortunate victim of a crash at one turn, when three chariots somehow touched each other at such a speed that all three spun horribly into the outside wall, a tangle of horses, chariots and men, dust clouding the scene. For a moment the crowd seemed to hold its collective breath until it became clear that miraculously no-one was hurt beyond being bruised and shaken and only one horse seemed injured. Attention quickly reverted to the remaining seven competitors. By the time they came past on the fifth lap, Flavius and Linnius were clearly in the lead and the rest were left some yards behind.

'Now we shall see a race!' Marcus delared gleefully, straining forward in anticipation while Thea, her voice hoarse from cheering, silently prayed that he might not suffer such a crash as Aulus. She did not need Marcus's comment to tell her that Linnius's team was tiring faster than Flavius's, for Linnius was using his whip freely and his horses were foaming more from their exertions. But, despite that, and despite his position on the inside, Flavius seemed unable to do more than edge a few feet ahead, only to have Linnius gain on him and take the lead again. The two chariots were frighteningly close to each other and the fierce rivalry between the two men was obvious.

'Oh, come on, come *on*!' Thea screamed, the strain and excitement almost too much to bear. 'Faster, faster!'

As they turned safely at the top of the curve to begin the last lap, Flavius began to pull ahead. Thea leaped up and down in undisguised glee. Marcus was also out of his seat, already anticipating victory. The noise reverberating around the stadium was deafening and everyone seemed to have forgotten the remaining competitors.

Flavius hugged the inside as they thundered into the final turn. Perhaps he tried to swing his speeding team too sharply around the tight bend, for they skidded badly, causing Thea to cry out in alarm and Marcus to forcibly declare Flavius a fool. Worse, the mistake, although quickly rectified, allowed Linnius to come again and as they swept into the final straight, he closed recklessly on Flavius's chariot, his lead horse now level with Flavius's back two. Flavius flicked his whip and drew ahead as the last turn and winning line loomed up.

What happened then was never exactly clear, although Marcus always maintained that it was quite clearly deliberate on the part of Linnius. Flailing wildly with his whip, Linnius pulled his chariot so close to Flavius that his leading horses almost brushed against the other team, and his wheels almost grazed the back of Flavius's chariot. The grey horses were pushed perilously close to the low wall of the spina, and the leading animal, obviously frightened, bucked and skidded, causing the team to bunch and collide, and the chariot, twisting violently round at the back, hit Linnius's chariot a glancing blow as it veered sharply away.

There was a ghastly, splintering sound and Flavius, pulling out his knife in a swift, instinctive movement, sliced through the harness of his panicking team. As the chariot snapped free, it lost a wheel and crashed violently onto its side, sliding across the track, turning over and coming to rest in pieces in the path of the approaching competitors, with Flavius pinned beneath it all.

CHAPTER NINE

THEA screamed. The crowd was on its feet and, after the initial gasp of horror, almost silent. Somehow, miraculously, the five other chariots managed to avoid the crumpled wreckage and hurtled on towards the winning line which Linnius had already crossed, virtually unnoticed.

Octavia began to weep hysterically; Thea stood rigid and appalled, gripping Marcus's arm convulsively and staring down at the scene in horror as the officials rushed out to lift the broken chariot from its trapped driver. 'He will be all right,' Marcus said quietly, but there was no real conviction in his voice and Thea scarcely heard him. They pulled the wreckage from Flavius's motionless body and as she watched them carry him away, unable to tell whether he was alive or dead, a suffocating dread crept over her and she began to tremble.

'Marcus, take Octavia and Thelia home.' Pontius's uncertain voice sounded far away and only her brother's hand on her arm made her drag her eyes from the sad little procession on the track below. Her father was already half-turned away, intent on hurrying down to follow them.

'I must go to him,' Octavia cried, her face deathly pale and her eyes wild with horror. 'I must go to him.' She began to follow her father, but he turned and stopped her, and there was a harrowing scene as she gave way to hysterics.

Thea was cold and trembling, a sick fear lying in the pit of her stomach. She watched, without really seeing, as Nero ordered his minions to find out what had happened, even as the starter and several officials were hastening towards the Emperor's canopy.

Eventually, Octavia's hysterics gave way to weeping and she was helped away by two servants. 'Come on,' Marcus said at Thea's shoulder, 'We must go home and wait. There is nothing we can do here.'

Reluctantly, Thea nodded, a hard lump rising in her throat and bringing the sting of tears to her eyes. 'Do you think he is—do you think—' She could not bring herself to finish, and Marcus could only shake his head.

They went home in virtual silence. Octavia was consigned to the care of her servant and Thea and Marcus sat down to wait. The wait was interminable and she could not keep still, pacing up and down in a torment of worry, chewing her lip and starting at every sound until Marcus was moved to insist that she sit down. 'I cannot! Suppose he is dead? Suppose . . .' She turned away and swallowed hard. 'Oh, why do they take so long?'

'Are you in love with him?' he demanded, surprised.

She swung round and stared at him. 'What do you mean?'

There was a bemused look in his eyes. 'You know Father wants you and Flavius to marry—' he began.

'Yes, yes,' she said impatiently, 'but it is impossible!'

'Why is it impossible? I think it would be—'

'Oh, be quiet!' she snapped suddenly, and turned abruptly away, her mind reeling. How could she talk about Flavius and her father's desire for her to marry him when he might be dead or horribly injured? 'I am going to my room,' she said, fighting back tears and hurried away before she broke down completely.

It was no better in her room. If anything, it was worse, for she did not have to pretend. She stood with her back to the door, her hands pressed against her cheeks. She loved him. She knew it with a certainty that settled on her like a skin. Now it was clear to her that Flavius, more than anything else, had been the reason she could not leave Rome, could not go with Gregor. It was a chilling knowledge, for ever since her arrival in Rome she had accepted that it was Octavia who commanded his real interest and involvement and nothing had altered that conviction. It was obvious from their stormy encounters that however Roman she became, he thought of her still as an Iceni savage and little more than a silly child. Certainly he would not countenance her as a wife. She paced up and down in a fever of anxiety, each minute seeming like an hour, her heart pounding painfully and every breath rasping with fear. She knew with horrible certainty that if he were dead, she would be unable to bear it.

When, finally, there was a jumble of sounds outside and Pontius's voice giving orders, she stared stupidly at the door, unable to move. The assortment of noises and indistinguishable words told her nothing and suddenly there was silence. She stood there for a moment, waiting for something to happen, someone to come. Then she threw open the door and stepped out into the marble and mosaic corridor; it was deserted.

A cold fear clutching at her throat, she went slowly to her father's study, where he and Marcus were standing by the table, talking in undertones. Pontius was holding Flavius's cloak. 'Father—?' she began, her voice dry and hesitant.

Pontius turned and smiled. 'He is all right, Thelia.'

'Oh.' Relief flooded through her and she put out a hand to steady herself against the door. 'Where—is he?'

'At home. They have taken him back to his own house.'

'Is he badly hurt?' she asked anxiously.

'He was very lucky. He has some bad cuts and bruises and—' the old man smiled, 'moving about is going to be painful for a few days. But he will survive.'

She turned quickly away, relief bubbling through her, bringing tears to her eyes. 'I'm—glad,' she said with difficulty, carefully averting her face. 'Has—anyone told Octavia. She seemed very upset.'

'Not yet,' Marcus said and grinned. 'It will do her good to fret for a while.'

'Marcus,' his father chided gently, 'go and tell her now, please. Thelia, perhaps you should rest before dinner. You look very pale.'

Thea bowed her head and murmured acquiescence, escaping gladly back to her room. She felt different, quite different. But nothing had really changed. Certainly she had acknowledged that she loved him—even now she was shaking with the relief of knowing he was alive and relatively unharmed. If he took her into his arms again and kissed her, she knew she would be unable to keep her feelings in check. She would beg him to take her, she would tell him she loved him and did not care about Octavia or any of the other women he was supposed to have had. But that was not what she wanted. She wanted him to *love* her. To need her. Only her, Thelia.

But what could she offer him when Octavia was so poised and beautiful and knowing?

* * *

MY DAUGHTER THELIA

There seemed no solution to her problem and her thoughts were full of Flavius all evening, wondering how he was, wondering how it had been between him and Octavia before he went to Britain. Presumably it was the scandalous talk about him and the demands of other women, which Octavia had told her was the cause of his departure for Britain, that had prevented their marriage. But now? Her head was reeling by the time she retired to her room to go to bed. Perhaps, when next she saw him, she would demand to know what he wanted of her, whether he was really just amusing himself and was only interested in adding her name to the list of noble-born Roman women he had taken to his bed, or whether there was something more behind the attention and the caresses.

She was preparing for bed and had just removed the new necklace and draped it over the arched back of the cat Flavius had given her, when there was a timid knock on the door. She called 'Enter' and Silla slid furtively into the room and stood with her back against the door. 'I am sorry to intrude, my lady, but a man has just come with a message for you.'

'A message? For me? But—'

'It is about the gladiator, Gregor.'

Thea frowned. 'Yes?'

'He is in some sort of trouble, my lady. The man said only that something had gone wrong and the gladiator needs some money very quickly. He begs that you go down to the waterfront and take as much money as you can. He seems very ashamed to ask it, and would not stay to see you himself because the gladiator had forbidden him to come and he dared not stay longer.'

Thea, stunned, was momentarily at a loss. What on

earth was she to do? 'He said I should go at once?' She felt vaguely irritated.

Silla nodded. 'He said he would have the gladiator meet you at the old corn warehouse. I can give directions,' she added.

Thea was silent for a moment. What else could she do? If Gregor was in some kind of trouble . . . A sudden thought struck her. 'Silla, do you know this man? Is he—' She searched for the word. 'Honest?'

'I know only that he is one of Tibelius's school, my lady; a gladiator, as Gregor is.'

Thea chewed her lip. Either he was Gregor's friend, or else he was up to something more devious; perhaps it was an attempt by Tibelius to trap Gregor? But that she dismissed impatiently. For one thing he probably would not go to so much trouble, and involving her in this way could not help anyway for she had no idea where Gregor was and the message did not seem designed to find out whether she knew or not. It was unlikely, too, that Tibelius knew anything about her, so how would the man have known where to come, unless he were trusted by Gregor?'

'Very well,' she said quickly, before her whirling thoughts grew any more confused, 'I will be ready in a few moments. Has Lucius locked the gates?'

'I don't think so. I will go and see.'

Thea changed her clothes and brought out her cloak and more robust sandals. She had a purse stuffed with coins but knew without counting that the collection of sesterces and denarii could not amount to enough to be of significance if Gregor was in real need. She pulled the strings of the purse closed with a sigh. It would have to do. Then the door opened and Octavia appeared, a startled expression on her face. 'Thelia, I have just seen

Silla. She told me—' Thea silently cursed. Of course Silla would have to tell her mistress! 'You are going?'

Surely it was obvious? 'Yes,' she said shortly.

'Thelia dear, I know I have not been very pleasant these past few days, but I have an atrocious temper and I am sorry for it, truly. Is there anything I can do to help?'

'No, thank you,' Thea said stiffly, 'Except not to tell anyone.'

'But you need money. Silla said—'

The younger girl hesitated. She did not trust this sudden change in Octavia, yet her sister was such a mercurial person her changes in humour were impossible to predict, and perhaps the shock she had received over Flavius had brought her to her senses. Her indecision must have been apparent in her face for Octavia said quietly, 'I will get what I have,' and disappeared, to return a few minutes later with two leather purses heavy with gold. 'Take these.'

Thea's eyes widened a little and a frown of suspicion wrinkled her brow. Was Octavia in the habit of hoarding such sums of gold? Or was the allowance Pontius gave her many times the amount he gave his youngest daughter? But Gregor needed money and here was surely enough for even the direst emergency. So she accepted gratefully. 'I will pay it back when I can,' she said, somewhat optimistically.

Octavia waved her silent. 'Wait while I get ready; I will come with you.'

'No!' Thea said quickly. 'Thank you, but it is not necessary.' Truthfully, though, she would have been glad of the company for the thought of walking all the way to the river in the dead of night was not a little daunting. However, some inner distrust made her wary and she thought she would be better alone.

Octavia, however, had other ideas. 'Don't be absurd! You cannot possibly go all that way alone in the middle of the night. Silla will go with you.'

She did not argue, and a few minutes later the two girls crept from the house and went silently through the garden to the dark street beyond. It was raining slightly and Thea huddled her cloak around her, clutching one of the purses of gold out of sight in its folds, whilst Silla carried Octavia's other purse. She was filled with doubts and fears. Was this a fool's errand? Some trick, perhaps? Warning voices in her mind persistently told her to go back, but she went on because there was as little proof to discredit Silla's story as there was to substantiate it.

The streets they took were deserted but for the silent cats that arched their backs against the walls as they left the houses and villas, the high ornate railings and the fountain-filled gardens of Rome's richest citizens and wove their way through damp and shadowy streets of poorer quarters. They avoided the small groups of young men happy with wine and unsteady on their feet, or solitary figures lurking in alleys and doorways, and only at a distance heard the occasional rattle of wheels or the clatter of a horse's hooves on the main thoroughfares. Otherwise there was an almost eerie silence, hollow and echoing between the blank-faced walls of the buildings that seemed to loom up on either side, punctuated only by a drip of rain from a roof or a tiny splash as their feet found small puddles between the stones.

It was a very long way, and the feeling that danger was lying in wait at every corner put a strain on her nerves. Every muscle ached by the time they began to smell the stale-corn and musty jute-sack odours of the warehouses.

Silla suddenly came to a stop and handed Thea the

purse she had been carrying, before softly calling a name into the darkness. The rain was a little heavier and Thea felt damp beneath her cloak, as she listened to the sound of water lapping gently against the wharves. Silla called again, a little louder, and this time several men emerged from the warehouse. Thea narrowed her eyes, scrutinising the figures for Gregor, but even in the darkness and at a distance she knew he was not there. A sick feeling of dismay stirred in the pit of her stomach. She knew she should not have come. She turned to the girl beside her. 'Silla—!' But Silla had gone, vanished into the night.

A wave of panic swept over her and she turned back to the men before her. 'Gregor?' Her voice was a harsh croak and she was answered only by sniggering laughter. Fear sent every coherent thought from her mind. She spun round and began to run, but clutching the heavy weight of gold made running difficult, and she was hampered by her long skirt and cloak and within a few moments the men were all around her. 'Where is Gregor?' she demanded stupidly, real panic in her voice now.

'Don't know the man,' one said with a solemn shake of his head, and grinned. 'Why don't you just give us the gold?'

'Why don't we just do it?' another hissed, a trace of urgency in his voice. 'Quick and quiet, like we were told.'

'Might as well have some fun first,' came the leering reply.

Thea looked desperately for a way out. She whirled round and swung a heavy purse into the face of the man nearest to her. As he screamed out in pain and shock, she kicked him hard and threw herself past him, running desperately towards the black void that was the entrance to an alley before the men behind her had a chance to recover. But she was quickly caught and overwhelmed, the gold wrenched from her grasp, and her cloak torn from her and flung aside. She struggled violently, cursing and screaming, her gown beginning to tear in their greedy hands. It was a nightmare. This could not be happening to her again, surely. Only last time Flavius had ridden up and saved her with one quiet word in his cool, commanding voice. But there was no Flavius this time.

'Flavius!' The cry for help was stifled as her hair was caught in grasping fingers, her legs buckling beneath her. Suddenly the breath was knocked from her body as she hit the ground with a force that sent a shooting, paralysing pain down her back. The face above her seemed horribly grotesque, and she turned her head away from his stinking breath, dimly aware of the heated argument of the other men and the chink of gold. Summoning the very last of her energy and resistance, she gasped in a mouthful of damp, cool air, threw every ounce of a strength she did not know she had into fighting. She writhed and twisted, lashed out and clawed at the face and the arms, blind with desperation.

She suddenly found herself on her side; instinctively her hands sought the wet stones and she thrust herself upwards until she was on her knees. Still fighting and struggling, she dragged her legs beneath her until her feet pressed on the ground, and managed to stagger a few steps, laughter and argument ringing in her ears and hands dragging at her arms and legs.

There was the sound of running footsteps and a harsh warning hiss of 'The vigiles! The vigiles are coming. Get it done and come away!'

Abruptly, she was dealt a cruel, cracking blow on the

back of her head which sent her sprawling to the ground again, pain splitting through her like a thousand hot knives, blinding her with a violent red blur that shattered into tiny fragments behind her eyes like splintered glass. Vaguely, she was aware that her attackers had fled because of the approach of the vigiles nocturni who patrolled the streets at night watching out for disturbances and that she was saved. But relief was momentary; the redness behind her eyes darkened and she collapsed, sinking into blackness.

She lay inert as the footsteps died away, the rain getting worse and seeping through her thin, torn gown. She came round, briefly, aware only of unbearable pain and a chilling dampness, and some tiny part of her mind still capable of thought told her that the vigiles had not come, that she had to move, to get up out of the rain, go home . . . Flavius. Flavius would help her. She would be safe with him, safe in his arms . . .

Somehow, she turned over, but the excruciating pain made it impossible for her to stand and she half-crawled, half dragged herself the short distance to a shadowy doorway. There, finally, the blinding pain overwhelmed her totally and she collapsed into oblivion.

CHAPTER TEN

FLAVIUS passed an extremely uncomfortable night. One leg was almost scraped raw, and both his arms were badly cut and bruised—indeed his whole body was covered in cuts and bruises and there was no position in which he was comfortable.

For him, it had been a week he would far rather not have gone through. The knowledge that Pontius nursed a desire for Thea and he to be wed had come as something of a shock—but not an unpleasant one. However, when she had made it clear that she wanted nothing to do with such a scheme, he had come home and got exceedingly drunk. The Emperor's sudden announcement of a chariot race had seemed a perfect outlet for the aggression and frustration burning in him. It also gave him a valid excuse to be absent from Rome for a week.

It was absurd that a mere chit of a girl could take such a hold on him as Thea had. She was little more than a child; temperamental, and unpredictable, stubborn, bewitching, disarmingly beautiful and innocently sensual. It had begun as an amusement, flirting with her and rousing her to stormy temper. But her anger and sparkling eyes had aroused more than amusement in him. Just lately it had been all he could do to keep from carrying her off into his bed and setting alive that sensual fire that seemed to be lurking somewhere behind those alluring, violet eyes, driving him insane. It was ridiculous. He,

Flavius, who had made love to some of Rome's richest and most beautiful women, was bewitched by the elfin face and vulnerability of a girl who seemed only to dislike and fear him. Oh, certainly her body responded to his touch, but it was not enough. It was her heart he wanted and that belonged to the Briton, Gregor.

It was Octavia's fault that things were such a mess. He was well aware that it was she who had fanned Thea's friendship with the gladiator and assisted their secret meetings. He had tackled her about it on several occasions but had received only evasive answers and denials in reply. Always she took advantage of being alone with him to wrap herself around him like a serpent and make amorous suggestions that were better suited to a brothel. There was an almost suppressed violence about Octavia that he found chilling. It had a great deal to do with why he had gone away to Britain when her ambitions to marry him had become so well known as to be acutely embarrassing.

He was sorely tempted to allow things to go on as they were, to tell Pontius that he would be more than happy to marry Thea. He knew Thea well enough to know that she would find it very difficult to refuse to do something her father so clearly wanted for her.

But he knew he would have to tell Pontius it was impossible, not only because of Thea's feelings, but because he also had come to realise that if he could not have her willingly, he would rather not have her at all. There was no point putting it off any longer. Already this past week at the villa he had drunk more than he cared to admit—the wine had not only deadened his senses but dulled his reflexes, causing him to be too slow to avoid Linnius's chariot. He knew he was fortunate to be alive. He would go this morning and talk to Pontius, before his preoccupation with Thea got him into more trouble. Then, well then he would go away somewhere for a little while.

It took him nearly an hour to get ready, even with the help of his servants, every movement jarring some bruised and tender part of his body. Lotions and ointments eased some of the pain but there was little he could do about the mess his face was in—a ragged cut over one eye, an angry gash and bruise along his cheekbone, and a scrape along his jaw that made even talking uncomfortable.

He was quite unprepared for the turbulent scene that greeted him when he arrived at Pontius's house. As usual he entered through the side gate into the courtyard, and there stopped short at the sight of Marcus shaking Octavia's servant girl, Silla, quite mercilessly.

'I want the truth,' he was saying menacingly. 'If not, I'll have you flogged and sold to a Greek sailor!'

The girl quailed but said insistently: 'I really *don't* know what has happened to her, sir.'

'If you don't believe I will do it,' Marcus went on through gritted teeth, 'you are mistaken. And Octavia will not be able to save you. Now—what do you—?'

'Marcus!' Flavius came forward as quickly as his injuries allowed. 'What is going on?'

A look of relief passed fleetingly across the boy's face. 'Flavius!' Then: 'You're a mess!' Almost immediately anxiety clouded his face again. 'Thelia has disappeared,' he said. 'Her bed has not been slept in and half her clothes are missing—and all her jewellery.'

Something tightened in Flavius's chest as Marcus continued: 'Silla here said someone brought a note for her late last night, which she took in to her. Apparently it was sealed and she *says* she does not know what was in

MY DAUGHTER THELIA 151

it, neither did she recognise the fellow who brought it. Father has found fifty gold pieces missing from his study and Octavia says twenty have gone from her room. *She* thinks Thelia has stolen the money and run off with the gladiator—when she went to see him after the Games he told her he had found a ship to take him to Britain and Octavia is convinced she is in love with him. I don't believe any of it and I think Octavia knows more than she will say. And whatever Octavia knows, Silla knows.'

Flavius, not as convinced as Marcus that the explanation of Thea's disappearance was nonsense, had a nagging fear in the pit of his stomach. Had her unhappiness in Rome driven her into the arms of the gladiator and a ship bound for what she still regarded as home? Grim-faced and tight-lipped, he turned to the shrinking girl. 'I am sure the Emperor will be able to devise something particularly unpleasant for you if you are lying,' he said coldly.

Silla squirmed fearfully in Marcus's grasp, eventually blurting out: 'I was ordered to tell the Lady Thelia that a man had come with a message that the gladiator was in trouble and needed money and she was to go to the waterfront to meet him.'

'And none of it was true?' Marcus demanded before Flavius could speak. 'There was no message from the gladiator?'

'I—I don't know. I don't think so. The Lady Octavia—she arranged everything. She just told me what to do.'

There was a momentary silence. 'What has she done?' Marcus said in a shocked tone, releasing Silla abruptly.

Flavius did not care to think, but, knowing Octavia had a hand in it, his fear deepened. 'Where is she?'

'Inside.'

Believing Octavia's theory that Thelia had run away with Gregor, Pontius had already despatched servants to the Emperor, and to Gregor's trainer Tibelius, and to that part of the city used by merchants and sea captains in an attempt to track down his runaway daughter before it was too late. He scarcely knew whether to be angry with Thelia or afraid for her.

'Where is Octavia?' Flavius demanded harshly.

Pontius looked startled to see him there, and alarmed at his tone.

'Where is she?' Marcus repeated. 'She has something to do with this.' Quickly he told his father what Silla had said and watched disbelief and bewilderment pass fleetingly across the old man's face.

'The girl must have misunderstood, there will be a reasonable explanation.' But he went to the door and bellowed 'Octavia!' in a voice Marcus had not heard him use for years.

'What is it?' she said, walking coolly into the room a moment later. 'Have you found her?' Her gaze alighted on Flavius and there was a flicker of surprise in her eyes. 'Flavius, dear! You look dreadful.'

Marcus whirled on her. 'Silla said you ordered her to tell Thelia that the gladiator was in trouble and needed money.'

'And you believed her?' she laughed. 'Marcus, really! How gullible you are. Obviously she is lying. Probably she helped Thelia to steal the money.'

'Silla would sell her soul for you,' he said, 'but there are a few things she is more afraid of than you, and we threatened her with them. She was not lying. What have you done?'

Octavia turned away, arrogance in every line of her

MY DAUGHTER THELIA

proudly erect body. 'This is absurd. Father you cannot allow him to speak to me like that.'

'I am aware how jealous of Thelia you have been,' Pontius said, 'You made that very clear to me only a few days ago. I think you had better answer Marcus.'

'I have done nothing,' she insisted. 'Is it my fault she was brought up as little more than a savage? You should not be surprised that she has run off with a gladiator. Sooner or later she was bound to do something like this. She has been meeting him secretly for weeks—'

'With more than a little help from you,' Flavius interrupted coldly. It was obvious to him, simply by the sparkle in her eyes and her defiant bearing that she was somehow responsible for Thea's disappearance—and not just by helping her to run away. 'We will get more out of Silla,' he said sharply and strode from the room, ignoring the darts of pain in his legs.

Silla was no longer in the servants' quarters and no-one had seen her since Marcus had dragged her out a few minutes earlier. He went back across the courtyard, frowning. As he re-entered the house, he turned towards Octavia's room. The door was slightly ajar and he pushed it wider to see Silla, kneeling with her back to him before a curtained recess, thrusting clothes from behind it into a sack. With a sharp intake of breath, he took two strides across the room and wrenched the sack from her hands, and shook out the contents. Thelia's clothes and jewellery, and the cat he had given her, tumbled out onto the floor.

Silla shrank away, but he hauled her to her feet and pushed her ahead of him to Pontius's study where Octavia was still protesting languidly that she had neither seen nor heard anything of Thelia since they had retired to bed the previous evening.

'I have just found Silla in Octavia's room,' he said grimly to Pontius. 'Thelia's clothes and jewellery are all there; they were hidden in the recess and this miserable little wretch was about to dispose of them.' He looked accusingly at Octavia, who had paled ever so slightly. She was looking venomously at the quailing girl, who suddenly blurted out: 'I am so sorry, my lady, but I was so tired when I got back I went straight to bed and—and I thought to get rid of it all this morning, but I didn't have time and—'

'Shut up, you fool!' Octavia snapped. 'Don't you realise you are getting yourself in even more trouble!'

'I am afraid it is you who are in trouble, Octavia,' Pontius said heavily. He turned to the trembling servant. 'You had better tell the truth, girl, if you wish to live. Where is my daughter?'

Silla's face crumpled in despair. 'I do not know, sir. I—I had only to give her the message and then take her to—to the old corn warehouses. A man would be there and I was then to come straight back. But there—there were three men, or four. I didn't wait . . .' Her voice trailed away as tears streamed down her face and she dropped to her knees, raising pleading eyes to Pontius. 'Forgive me, sir. I had no choice. Please—'

Impatiently, Pontius waved her silent. 'Octavia, what have you done?' he demanded, forcing the words with unsteady voice, 'What have you done?'

'I have rid us of her!' she declared with malicious triumph, her eyes over-bright and an ugly twist to her mouth. 'And you will never have your wish now! Flavius will never marry her now.' She looked up at Flavius and laughed. 'You would never have got that sweet little virgin into your bed outside marriage—you ought to thank me!'

MY DAUGHTER THELIA

But Flavius's face had set into rigid lines, his eyes glinting dangerously. 'If you have—'

'It's her own fault,' she said carelessly, ignoring him and dropping into a chair, curling one arm up around her head and letting the other trail carelessly down the side. 'I went to a lot of trouble to help her meet that gladiator. *I* thought she was in love with him and would be only too happy to go back to Britain with him. It cost me a great deal of money to pay that captain to take her too. And then she said she did not want to leave Rome . . . And then *you*,' she turned venomous eyes on her father, 'You said you planned for her to marry Flavius. He is mine, you know that!'

She turned away and was silent a moment, then looked up at Flavius. 'You should never have brought her here,' she said reprovingly. 'You should never have gone to Britain at all. You should have stayed here and married me. Everyone expected it. But now Thelia has gone—'

Flavius sprang forward and grasped her arm, wrenching her to her feet. 'You are insane! What have you done?'

She pulled away and stared resentfully at him. 'I sent her off to meet a very disreputable sailor,' she said sitting down again, 'and gave her enough gold to pay him well for relieving us of her!' She looked up at her father and smiled a little regretfully at the expressions of horror and shock on his face. 'I am sorry you know the truth. Had this—slut—' she cast a glance full of disgust at Silla, 'obeyed her orders properly and kept her mouth shut, you would have believed that she had stolen the money and run away with her gladiator and was now on her way back to Britain.'

'I am going to the warehouses,' Flavius began, turning

away, but Pontius delayed him. His voice was laden with the weight of Octavia's awful confession and the horror of what may have happened to Thelia as he groped for a chair and sank into it.

'Who is this man? Where can he be found? What exactly did you tell him—to do?'

'It's no use, Father,' she said in the tone of a patient adult addressing a slow-witted child. 'He was sailing for Egypt at first light today. I told him she would have seventy or eighty gold pieces on her and he could have them, and her, as long as we never saw her again. I imagine he's far out at sea by now with Thelia well and truly his concubine. So you see,' she added sweetly, 'even if you found her and brought her back, Flavius,' she glanced round at him, 'would not marry her. She might even now be carrying a sailor's child! No-one would ever marry her.'

'But there were three or four men,' the now thoroughly frightened Silla put in, 'not one as you said.'

Octavia shrugged. 'He probably did not keep his mouth shut.'

Pontius, ashen-faced, could only look blankly at her, appalled, and Flavius, his mind racing, felt sick with revulsion.

'You have sent Thelia to her death!' Marcus shouted and sprang forward, rage and anguish overwhelming him. Flavius pulled him back.

'Time for that later,' he said tersely. 'Come, we must go down to the old warehouses, there may be something . . .' He paused and looked at Pontius. 'Will you stay here and wait? She may have escaped; she has a lot of courage and she is very resourceful. Someone should be here.'

Pontius seemed to have recovered slightly. 'Yes, yes.

Go quickly. Someone will be here from the Palace soon I expect.' On the way out, Flavius instructed Lucius to fetch two other servants and stay with Octavia and under no circumstances to allow her to leave the house.

'Use force if necessary, and look to your lives if she escapes!'

Heedless of the discomfort and pain his injuries were causing him, Flavius became more and more grim-faced as they hurried through the city at breakneck speed. His thoughts turned this way and that over the deeper implications of what Octavia had done.

He knew only too well that a common sailor would not be able to take a girl on board ship and would be far more likely to rape her—then kill her, take the gold and dump her body in the river. It was an impossible hope that he had been blinded by the gold and, instead of sailing with his ship, had taken Thelia somewhere to use as he pleased and had not killed her. If he had had dealings with Octavia, he would know better than to stay in Rome. And if there were three or four of them—it was too horrible to imagine.

His anguish was made worse by a deep sense of guilt. He should have guessed, should have realised that Octavia was up to something. He had known her long enough and should have suspected that lurking insanity. He had known that she was helping Thea meet the gladiator—he surely should have known that Octavia rarely did anything out of the goodness of her heart and that by encouraging her young sister's association with the Briton, she was only furthering her own ends. If anything had happened to her, to his dear, funny little Thea, he would never forgive himself. And try as he might he could find little cause for optimism in his heart.

But even in his anxiety and despair, he knew they

were *all* to blame. Thea's sudden appearance in Rome had made her the centre of attention. Everyone from Nero down had doted on her, given her presents, spent time with her; friends, neighbours, acquaintances had been curious and attentive and Octavia, hitherto very much the darling of Rome and the only daughter of a doting, indulgent father, suddenly found herself in the shadows. It was not something the vain, self-centred Octavia would have taken lightly.

The main cause of her jealousy, of course, was the attention *he* had been paying Thea. He had been close to marrying Octavia at one point—everyone had thought they would, but her selfishness and constant demands on his attention and his time had eventually brought him to his senses and, tired of Rome and bored with Octavia, he had requested the Emperor to find him some position with the army far enough away to render him safe from Octavia. Vastly amused Nero had obligingly sent him to Britain, the farthest-flung corner of the Empire. He had found on his return that she was still determined to marry him, and keeping away from her when Thea was under the same roof had proved impossible. He knew she was jealous of course, but how could he—or anyone—have known that her jealousy would drive her to the edge of madness, that she would go so far . . . ?

Quite what he expected to find at the old corn warehouse, or along the busy wharves and moorings, he did not know. But they found nothing. They questioned everyone they met—ancient, wizened sailors and scruffy ragged children; old women, grimy and hostile, and scantily clad girls straying from the brothels for a breath of morning air. No-one had seen anything of the beautiful young girl they described, or heard anything unusual—though nothing was 'unusual' in that part of the

MY DAUGHTER THELIA

city. A girl's screams were common enough in the middle of the night and a girl in the company of several men was scarcely likely to raise an eyebrow. Who could tell whether the girls were willing or unwilling anyway?

They were forced to give up their fruitless search eventually and return, silent and drawing little comfort from the fact that at least they had not found a body, to the oppressive atmosphere of Pontius's house. They were greeted with the news that Nero himself had only just left, having put a number of his personal servants at the disposal of his friend, sending them about the city to make enquiries, and to Ostia harbour for news of ships sailing for Egypt. In order to avoid Octavia's part in her sister's disappearance becoming known and creating a hideous scandal these servants were told only that the lady Thelia had vanished and was believed kidnapped.

Octavia, for the time being, had been locked in her room and Pontius could only sit with shoulders sagging, shaking his head in grief and despair. The servant he had sent to Tibelius when he believed Thelia had run away with Gregor, had returned to say that the gladiator had not escaped. It appeared that the ship had been delayed for several days and Tibelius, knowing nothing of Gregor's plan, was most grateful for the information and now had Gregor locked up while he decided what to do with him.

Flavius, when he heard this, got warily and painfully to his feet. 'There is something I can do, then,' he said, his voice leaden and expressionless, and he left the hushed, shattered gloom of the house.

All the way to Tibelius's training school, Flavius's thoughts were heavy; and, whenever they dwelt on Octavia, almost murderous. His limbs ached and his bruises throbbed. He alighted from the litter in a leaden mood, his cold, commanding tone brooking no argument when he demanded to see Tibelius. Tibelius was not amused at being drawn away from the training rituals of his 'familia' but, with grudging deference, led Flavius to the privacy of a dingy little room littered with gladiatorial trappings.

'One of your men,' Flavius said abruptly, 'Gregor. I want him released.' He tossed a purse of gold on the table. 'That should be more than sufficient.'

Tibelius looked at him distrustfully, and picked up the purse, weighing it thoughtfully in one hand. 'Why?'

'That is none of your concern.'

Tibelius shrugged. 'He's no use to me now. Sejanus should have had him the last time. You can take him.' He led Flavius to a locked door down the corridor, which he unbolted and ordered Gregor out. Surprise registered on the Briton's face at the sight of Flavius. 'You're free,' Tibelius said flatly, and, leaving the two of them standing there, went back to his training.

'I have bought your freedom,' Flavius explained to the bewildered Gregor. 'Come outside.'

'Why?' Gregor demanded suspiciously as they emerged into daylight. 'Did Thea ask—'

'Thea is—' he hesitated and then said flatly: 'Thea has disappeared, very probably sent to her death by her own sister.'

'But—' Gregor began, shock evident in his expression. 'I don't—'

From the litter, Flavius took another heavy purse. 'There is nothing you can do. Take this and go home. I believe your ship sails in the morning.'

Gregor made no move to take the purse. 'But—'

Flavius looked at him and his voice was heavy. 'We do

not know where she is or what has happened to her, but it is more than likely that she is dead. Everything possible is being done.' He put the purse in the other man's hand. 'Take it before I change my mind.' He turned stiffly towards the litter, but Gregor stopped him.

'Why? Why are you doing this?'

He sighed heavily. Why indeed? 'But for me, she would still be safe with the Iceni; cold and hungry perhaps, but alive. This is the least I can do for her.' He turned away again. 'You are a free man. Tibelius will sort out the formalities. Go home.' He got into the litter awkwardly and instructed the slaves to take him home, leaving Gregor standing there looking after him.

When he arrived home, he sent a messenger to Pontius for news. There was none. After allowing the dressings on the worst of his cuts and scrapes to be changed, and ointments to be rubbed into the ghastly, throbbing bruises, he slumped into a chair and sent both his solicitous servants and his unappetising supper away, remaining with a flagon of wine in the creeping darkness. He ached all over. What did not ache because of the chariot crash ached with weariness. What evil gods had possessed him to bring Thelia back to Rome? He had not quite given up hope, but the chances of finding her alive were so remote that it was a self-indulgence to cling to it. He should have stayed in Britain and left Thea there too. Ironic that she should have survived kidnap, violence and rebellion, Roman cruelties, cold, hunger and loneliness with scarcely a scar, only for a comparatively few months in the bosom of her family, ensconced in the luxury of Rome, to send her to a cruel and violent death, betrayed by her own sister.

As the darkness closed in on him, so did his guilt and the effects of the wine. He fell asleep with a lingering picture of her on that distant moor where he had first seen her, the sun spinning gold in her tangled mass of hair, her dark blue eyes sparkling with anger and fear, her thin body trembling. The tunic had been revealingly torn down at the neck and even then he had been tempted . . .

It was just light when a horrified servant, entering the room to tidy up before his master rose, found him still there and woke him. Half an hour spent gingerly in the baths, whilst easing a little the aches and stiffness worsened by his night in the chair, did little to dispel the numbness that seemed to have settled on his mind.

He was barely dressed when a commotion at the door sent him to investigate, irritation creasing his brow and a sharp rebuke on his lips. He was startled to find his servant trying to refuse entry to a large woman of indeterminate years and unmistakable profession. She was over-dressed and painted and was possessed of a loud and penetrating voice which demanded to speak to Flavius.

'What is it?' he snapped, in pain and in no mood for irrelevancies.

'You Flavius?' The woman pushed her way in and stood looking round with undisguised curiosity, eventually turning her eyes on him. 'Meet someone unpleasant on a dark night, did you?' she chuckled, nodding towards his battered face, but when he did not answer, she went on quickly: 'She didn't *look* like she was anybody—not like she'd come from a place like this. But then she didn't look like anythin' much, come to think of it.'

'What are you talking about woman?' There was a sharp edge in his voice, and his throat was dry with sudden anticipation.

'Well now, she said only a few words, see. Kept sayin' "Flavius" and somethin' about gladiators and messages. So I thought Flavius was a gladiator, see. Spent the whole afternoon askin' round, I did, 'til eventually I sees this trainer, Tibelius.' She squared her shoulders in satisfaction, which lifted her ample bosom and added a new dimension to her extravagant figure.

'And?' Flavius prompted impatiently.

'He says there's been an almighty fuss about a girl gone missin' and that she's probably the daughter of Pontius somethin' or other, and that a Flavius had been to see him only that very afternoon. Well, I found out where you lived, but there weren't much point comin' last night. I had to get back to see she was all right and I got business to attend to. So here I am. Didn't fancy goin' to that Pontius—she might've run away from him for all I know an' it were Flavius she were askin' for.'

Flavius managed to interrupt this flow long enough to demand: 'You have Thea? Is she all right? Why did you not bring her here with you, woman?'

'Well, now,' she put her hands on rounded hips and looked at him almost pityingly. 'I don't know her *name*. Got red hair, sort of. Funny colour really. And as for bein' all right, she's alive, if that's what you mean. Said a few words when we got her into bed—yesterday mornin' that'd be, after we found her down at the warehouses. Not said a word since, just lays there, sleepin' like. But she won't be woke up. Soaked through, she was—looked like she'd been layin' in the rain all night. Nasty couple of cracks on the head too, bruises on her face and arms, dress all torn . . .' She paused. 'Can't afford fancy physicians,' she declared defensively, 'but we done our best!'

'Ye gods, woman!' he exclaimed, ignoring the last

comments and finally giving vent to his exasperation. 'Don't you realise we have been worried sick! The Emperor's own servants have been out searching—'

'Well, what would I want talkin' to people like that?' she chuckled. 'Now are you comin' to fetch her or not? I really can't be doin' with her layin' there like that in my place, you know, an' as I said I can't afford fancy physicians an' the like—'

'Yes, yes. I'll come at once . . .' Caution prevented him sending someone to Pontius. It was still very early and it could, after all, be a mistake. So he took only two slaves bearing a litter and accompanied the woman through the city.

When he arrived at the dingy little house and climbed the narrow flight of stairs wincing at every step, he was moved to thank the gods that Thelia had fallen into the hands of an honest woman. What a temptation such a beautiful young girl would be to someone unscrupulous or in need of money. Sold as a slave she would surely have cost some rich travelling merchant or foreign noble a vast sum. Perhaps it was not so much honesty as a fear of the girl dying that had motivated the woman.

But when she opened the door of the gaudy little room, it was empty. A narrow bed was slightly crumpled, as if someone has lain in it, but of Thea there was no sign. The woman was obviously shocked and stared around the room in open-mouthed wonder. 'Why, she must've woke up and—'

Flavius swore in disbelief at her stupidity. 'Did you leave no-one with her?' he demanded.

'I didn't see no need. I only went out once last night and then I was in all night—'

'Did you come into this room after you came back?' he demanded.

'No, but—'

'Well, did you see her this morning before you came to me?'

'N-No—' There was fear in the woman's eyes now. 'I came straight—Well, it weren't as if there was no-one here!' she protested defensively. 'I left the girl downstairs to see to her if she needed anything.'

The young girl, little more than a child, could only say that there had been no sound from the room and she had seen no-one leave the house. But when Flavius questioned her closely, it turned out that she had not looked in on the sick girl at all, and that she had gone out herself soon after the older woman had left this morning and then she had only been gone an hour. That however, was two hours ago.

Flavius questioned everyone he could find, but no-one had seen a young girl leave the house. There was such a maze of narrow streets and alleyways in that area that it would be very easy to slip away unseen. Someone had seen a man with a mule and cart outside late last night, but there was nothing particularly untoward about it, and he had not seen a girl.

Sickened by the stupidity of the woman, Flavius could only hope that Thea had indeed come round and thought herself in danger, and finding herself alone had contrived to slip unseen from the house to try to make her way home. There was no alternative now but to go to Pontius and hope that if Thea was not already there, she would soon turn up. That, however, assumed that the young girl's assertion was correct that there had been no sound or movement from the room during the night. There was, however, a sick anxiety in his stomach and he could not help but think of several other less attractive possibilities.

Thea was not at the house when Flavius arrived there. Anxious to avoid upsetting Pontius any more than was necessary, he refrained from telling the old man about his early morning visitor and the possibility that Thea had been at her house last night. But when, after half an hour, she still had not appeared, he had to give up any faint hopes he had been nursing that she *would* turn up.

Suddenly, into his despair, came a thought of Gregor. The woman had said she had asked around all afternoon before seeing Tibelius, so she could not have been there very long after he himself had left. If the gladiator had not immediately departed for Ostia, and if he had seen the woman, or Tibelius had told him . . . He pulled himself to his feet and saying only that he would be back as soon as possible he left the house and went swiftly to Tibelius's training school once more.

There he discovered that Gregor had left the previous evening with a mule and a cart and that he had been going to Ostia. Someone had seen a mule and a cart outside the woman's house late last night! He had to go to Ostia. But the ship was due to sail that morning. If nothing delayed it, he would be too late. He sent the litter-bearers back to Pontius with a message that he was going to Ostia, then borrowed the best of the horses Tibelius kept for the gladiatorial contests.

He had to have help to mount the creature, and Tibelius clearly thought he was mad to attempt to ride at all in his condition. But something *may* have delayed the ship and he had to try. It would waste too much time to send to Pontius . . .

It was eighteen miles or so to Ostia. Every stride the horse took jarred his body horribly, sending shudders of pain through every bone; but he gritted his teeth and rode as fast as he could, his thoughts in such torment he scarcely noticed that the binding round his left arm was stained with blood again.

The gods were very unkind. He had finally acknowledged that he loved her only to fear that she was dead, then to discover that she was alive, but probably on her way to Britain with a man *he* had set free, her passage paid for with his own gold! The irony of it tasted bitter in his mouth. If he discovered in Ostia that she had not gone willingly with Gregor, he knew that he would follow them to Britain and claim her back. He could not live with his guilt in Rome, could not face life in that turbulent, vibrant city without her, tormented by the knowledge that she might be desperately unhappy and suffering any amount of hardship, and all of it his doing.

CHAPTER ELEVEN

THEA was aware first of a dreadful headache, and then of motion, an uneven jolting motion that jarred every aching bone in her body. Then there was a strange, squeaking-wood sound and a rumbling that vibrated all through her. And a smell, a warehouse smell of sacking. She lay perfectly still and began to remember. Those men . . . Silla running off . . . the gold . . . Gregor, not there . . . someone saying they had been told to do it 'quick and quiet'. A pang of fear—where was she now? She dared not move or speak out, but gingerly opened her eyes and found herself staring up at a grey-blue sky, the silver of early morning. Slowly she lowered her eyes to look down the length of her, and realised that she was in a cart lying beneath a rough blanket, on top of which were several sacks. Clearly they were outside the city for she could not see any buildings through the crack in the side of the cart, only trees and open ground.

She was too afraid to try to move round and see who was driving the cart, so she closed her eyes and remained still. But the motion of the cart and the throbbing of her head caused her stomach to churn horribly. After a little while she could no longer quell the rising nausea, and twisted onto her side, retching horribly. Her stomach was empty, however, and she fell back gasping as the gripping pains subsided.

The cart stopped. 'Thea?'

She opened her eyes and turned towards the familiar voice. 'Gregor! What are—?'

'Hush! You've had a bad time. Here—' He climbed up into the cart beside her and helped her sit up, holding a leather bottle of water to her lips. 'Are you all right?' he asked in his own language as he put the bottle down again.

'Yes. So you did send the message.'

He looked at her blankly. 'Message?'

She frowned, still a little muzzy-headed. 'Silla told me someone had come with a message from you—'

'Wait a minute. Can you ride at the front with me? We have to go on.'

She felt very weak and tired, and heavy-limbed, unable to think clearly, but she nodded anyway. With his help she got down and went round to the front of the cart where he had to lift her up onto the seat. The blanket was wrapped round her like a shawl and he put an arm around her, holding her close to him while he guided the mule with the rein held in his other hand. 'Now, what about a message?'

Slowly, struggling to remember, she told him what had happened, fighting a growing desire to sleep.

'I warned you about Octavia,' he said grimly. 'Flavius said she sent you to your death.'

Thea sighed heavily; it certainly seemed like that, but it was too much to think about now. 'How did *you* find me?' she asked him, struggling to clear her head of the fog.

'Your father sent a servant to Tibelius asking about me, with a story—Octavia's doing no doubt—that you and I had run off together. Tibelius found me preparing to escape, and locked me up. I could find no way out and thought myself lost. The ship was due to sail this morning and Tibelius was certain either to sell me or have me killed. Then your Flavius arrived, yesterday afternoon. He seemingly gave Tibelius enough gold to persuade him to let me go.'

Thea pulled herself out of her drowsiness. 'Why?'

'That is what I asked him. He said you very probably were dead and that but for him you would still be safe with the Iceni. Sending me home a free man was the least he could do. He gave me a thousand sesterces, too.' He was silent for a moment, then continued.

It seemed that when Gregor returned from making preparations for his journey to Ostia—buying the mule and food and a few clothes—Tibelius had a woman with him. He was telling her that perhaps the sick girl she had found was Pontius Aquila's missing daughter, and the Flavius she was enquiring about was the same one who had been to see him earlier. Tibelius told her where they both lived and the woman complained that she had no time to go trailing all that way at that time of day, but she would see to it in the morning. Gregor had followed her and when he knew where she lived, went back, packed up his mule and borrowed a cart. It was dark by then and, leaving the cart in an alley, he had watched the house until the woman had gone out, then slipped in and brought Thea out without being seen.

'She said you were sick,' he went on, 'but when I saw you lying there like death, I almost did not dare move you. But I could not leave you either. If your own sister plots your death, there is nothing these murdering Romans will not do! The sooner we sail home the better.'

Thea had grown drowsy and was fighting to understand what he was saying to her. 'Where—are we going?'

He turned his head to look at her in some surprise. 'To

Ostia, of course. The ship sails on the next tide. We should have plenty of time.'

'Ostia? But—'

'Try to sleep, Thea, you need rest. We will eat later.'

It was wrong. She did not want to go to Ostia. Gregor was taking her to Britain, but she did not want to leave Rome. She could not clear her mind of the foggy confusion, nor keep her eyes open. Finally she slumped against him, unable to fight the need for sleep any longer.

It was fully light and a cool breeze was blowing into her face when he gently woke her. She looked round in some alarm at the vast harbour spread before her. Ostia!

'Gregor, I cannot go with you,' she said. She sat up and ran her fingers through her tangled hair, pausing to touch gingerly the lump at the back of her head where the hair was matted with blood. A swift glance downwards gave her a sinking feeling of dismay: her crumpled gown was filthy and torn, and she noticed for the first time that her feet were bare.

'Don't be ridiculous,' he said, reaching for a small bundle of food, which he passed to her. 'You told me before that you did not want to leave Rome. I know that was for my benefit, and I couldn't take you anyway. It was unlikely that *I* would get to Britain alive and taking you was impossible. Now I have Flavius's money and I am a free man. We can go home together and in comfort.'

'I belong *here*,' she said, eating ravenously. 'This is my home now. I do not wish to go to Britain.'

'Your family has tried to kill you!' he said impatiently. 'I am taking you home.'

'I am sorry, truly,' she said with a mouthful of tasteless meat, 'but you must take me back. They will all be very worried if that woman went to tell Father where I was.'

He looked at her and when she raised her eyes to his, she was startled to see anger in them. 'Well, it's too late. The ship sails with the tide. Hurry and eat and we will go. I have to find where she's moored and arrange things.'

'No!' She flung away the meat and a tiny pang of fear jolted her heart. 'I am not going with you. You must go, of course, but I am going back to Rome.'

He laughed, rather harshly. 'On your own?'

She thrust her tangled hair off her face. 'Gregor, please. I want to go home. To Rome, to my family, to Fla—'

'Flavius!'

'Yes.' She drew a breath and plunged on desperately. 'Yes. We—we are to be wed.' And before he could stop her, she moved quickly and jumped from the cart, steadying herself against the side as a wave of dizziness swept over her. He was beside her in a moment, drawing her into his arms. She did not have enough strength to do more than push ineffectually against him.

'Thea, you must come with me. I love you. I need you. I have no-one in Britain. Come with me, come with me, Thea—' He was suddenly covering her face and hair with kisses, pleading with her. She could take no more, and crumpled against him, tears streaming down her face and long, shuddering sobs escaping her.

He grew still, and then pushed her away, holding her at arm's length, and looking down at her. 'Thea—'

'Let me go,' she whispered brokenly. 'Let me go back. I cannot fight any more, but I want to go back . . .'

There was a long silence between them. People went by giving them little more than a cursory glance. 'I cannot let you go back alone,' he said eventually. 'Come, we will find an inn and perhaps I can find someone to take you back safely.'

She nodded, allowing him to lead her away from the cart. She did not trust him and began to panic that he planned to force her to go. The events of the past few days had left her inwardly shaking with fear and unwilling to trust anyone easily. Too clearly she remembered giving in to sickness and weariness and allowing Flavius to take control of her—then she had found herself on a ship bound for this very harbour. She had no intention of allowing the same thing to happen in reverse. So she pulled her wits together and stopped, swaying a little. 'Let me wait here, Gregor. I do not think I can walk and I feel very dizzy. I must sit down. And eat. I'll wait here for you.'

He was reluctant, but she did not have to try to feign her pallor or unsteadiness, it was real enough. After a moment he agreed. 'All right. I'll not be very long.'

She nodded and leaned thankfully against the wooden cart, breathing heavily and feeling far from well as she watched him walk away. She did not have very much time. As soon as he was out of sight she gathered up what was left of the food, threw the blanket across the mule and unhitched the creature from the cart. Then, summoning what was left of her strength, she managed to pull herself on to its back, almost passing out with the effort and uncomfortably aware of the bruises on her arms. Fortunately, it was an amenable animal and moved off at her bidding, turning to go back the way they had come, and at a reasonable speed.

She prayed that Gregor would be gone long enough to enable her to go some distance, far enough to make it impossible for him to catch up with her on foot. Perhaps she was doing him an injustice, perhaps he really did intend to find someone to escort her home, but the risk seemed too great. That look in his eyes was somehow threatening, and she dared not trust him . . . But he wanted to get away from Rome far more than he wanted her, and if she could only go far enough before he realised she had gone, she was sure he would not risk the ship sailing without him.

She lost track of distance and time. The road ahead of her blurred and swayed, and came clear again, and her hold on consciousness grew more tentative. She knew she must eat, but would not stop yet; when she was sure, then she would stop.

Someone was coming towards her. She put a hand up to rub her eyes and tried to make out the figure. An old man, walking and leading a mule pulling a laden cart. She would ask him to help her. As he grew closer, she struggled hard to keep her grip on the mule and force her eyes to stay open, to shake the creeping mists from her wits, but the road, the old man, the trees, all began to merge into a swirling greyness she could no longer fight off, closing in on her until, as the old man drew level, she lost the battle completely and slipped from the mule to fall, with a sickening thud, onto the dusty road.

It was well into the afternoon when Flavius arrived in Ostia. And it took him only a few minutes to establish that the only ship going to Britain was still in the harbour. 'That ship!' laughed the wizened old man he had asked, as he pointed the vessel out to him. 'It'll be the work of the gods if *that* ship *ever* sails out of here!'

'Why?' he demanded. 'What's wrong?'

'What's *right* you mean. Her master's a villain and there's been trouble over her for days—supposed to sail this mornin' in the end but the master was dead drunk in the inn here and they missed the tide. Should sail on the next one, though. Did you want a passage? I think he's got one traveller already but I expect he'd take another for a price.

'No,' Flavius said, his heart sinking at the 'one' traveller. 'I do want to see the passenger he already has, though. Is he on board?'

'Don't think so.' The old man chuckled. 'I should think he's passing the time in the inn. Plenty of willing girls here for a man to spend a few hours with! I'd ask in there if I was you.'

Flavius limped across to the inn he had indicated, already acknowledging that it was probably futile. If Thea was not with Gregor now, she probably never had been and the mule and cart was a mere coincidence. After all, there must be hundreds of them in Rome. But it could do no harm to ask.

The inn boasted only two private rooms—usually taken by nobles or rich merchants and the innkeeper did not hesitate to tell Flavius that he had been suspicious of the Briton immediately—such men did not usually have the money to pay for a room. However, it was not his business to ask questions. Yes, as far as he knew, he was in the room now, and alone. No, he had not seen a girl with red hair.

Gregor was more than a little surprised to see him, and immediately asked if he had found Thea.

Flavius shook his head and sat down, passing his hand over his eyes wearily. 'I thought she would be with you.'

'What made you think that?' Gregor asked guardedly.

Flavius looked up at him, his eyes narrowing slightly. Despite his weariness and anxiety, and the throbbing of his aching body, he did not miss the slight tautness in the other man's tone. 'You have seen her.' It was more an accusation than a question.

Gregor nodded. 'Yes, I have seen her.' And he told Flavius briefly how he had found Thea and brought her to Ostia. 'But she would not come with me. After all you have done to her she must be insane to want to stay here! I went to the inn to try to find someone to take her back to Rome—the ship was about to sail, or so I thought, and I was not about to miss it because of her stupidity. I asked about the ship—I was gone longer than I expected, and when I came back she had taken the mule and gone. There was no sign of her along the road and I couldn't hope to catch her on foot.' He shrugged. 'As it happens I'm stuck here 'til the next tide. But there was nothing I could do about Thea. She's probably at home by now.'

Flavius leaped to his feet, fury blazing in his eyes. 'Ye gods, man! Didn't you even try to find her? Anything could have happened to her!'

'Not much is likely to have happened to that one!' Gregor said firmly. 'She was clever enough to fool me into thinking she was barely able to stand and then rode off with the mule as soon as my back was turned.'

Flavius, speechless with disbelief at what he was hearing, knew that he would probably murder the man if he stayed any longer. He strode to the door. 'If anything has happened to her, you had better be gone before I get back,' he said through gritted teeth. He left the inn quickly, shaking off his weariness, and went back to his horse. He had not passed her along the road, so it was fairly certain that she had not got back to Rome. A girl alone with a mule, a girl with a mass of hair the colour of hers would not easily pass unnoticed. Someone must have seen her.

The traffic was already lessening, and Flavius went some distance along the road, asking everyone he met if they had seen a beautiful young girl with dark red hair; looking in every ditch and behind every rock for some sign of her, or the mule. Something, anything . . . Ostia ended in a trickle of houses and villas, finally falling away to leave the road to Rome merely dotted with the occasional dwelling, and by the time Flavius reached what he knew to be the last place along the road before the outskirts of Rome, it was growing towards dusk and he had almost given up in despair. He knew he would have to rest soon, or else drop with exhaustion. He had eaten nothing since—He could not even remember when he had last eaten. And the bandage on his arm was now soaked with blood and the arm throbbed dully.

Yet still he maintained a lingering hope. True, he had not passed her on the way down, but he had passed any number of carts, covered wagons, litters . . . and there was the river—or she could still be sheltering in Ostia itself. She might even, by now, be safe at home. There were a dozen possibilities. Yet the dangers to a young girl travelling that road alone, especially one who might not be at all well or able to defend herself, did not bear thinking about.

'I am looking for a young girl,' he said mechanically to the elderly man who answered his knock. 'She was coming from Ostia with a mule. She may be hurt. She has red hair and—'

'Yes!' the old man cried. 'Yes, such a girl is here.' And then, suddenly grave, 'You do not look at all well yourself, sir. Your arm . . . Come in, come in.'

Flavius stared at him blankly for a moment, scarcely taking in what he had said, and the old man had to take his arm and draw him into the dim interior.

* * *

Thea lay in the little bed, drowsing but unable to sleep. She wanted to go home, but the old couple would not hear of it until morning. She had told them who she was and that her family believed she was dead, but she had been unconscious until well into the afternoon and the old man had said it was too late to go to Rome and anyway she was too weak to travel. They would go as soon as it was light in the morning, he said.

So she had eaten the steaming broth and tried to sleep. But it had been impossible, and her thoughts had darted this way and that trying to piece together what had happened to her. The message Silla had given her from Gregor was a fabrication by Octavia it seemed. But why? Had Octavia really planned to have her killed like that? Was she really so jealous? Thea could not bring herself to believe it, and yet, when she looked back over things—

She wanted to go home. To see Flavius, to feel his safe, strong arms around her, holding her close, protecting her. She knew he would melt the chill of loneliness that had settled around her heart. If only he truly loved her.

When she heard the knock, and the voices in the other room, she roused herself to listen. Was it her imagination, or was there really something familiar about the voice? She threw back the covers and got up, pausing a moment as a wave of dizziness washed over her, and then walked barefoot to the door, where she stood and listened. Her heart skipped a beat. Flavius! It *was* Flavius!

Heedless that she was clad only in a scanty shift, she threw open the door and saw him standing with the old man by the fire. There was such a welling up of emotions inside her at the sight of him that tears sprang into her eyes and for a moment she could not move.

'Thea!' The sound of his voice, and the relief in it, was enough. 'Thea—'

In another moment she was across the room and into his arms, the tears streaming uncontrollably down her face, unable to speak for the sobs that wracked her.

He pulled her tightly against him, covering her face and her hair with kisses. 'Thea, my love, my love,' he whispered into her hair, scarcely aware of what he was saying. 'You are safe. You are safe now, little one. I'll never let you out of my sight again. Whatever possessed you to go off on such a fool's errand in the middle of the night? Hush now. It's over and you're safe. I'll take you home now—'

'Sir, it's late,' the old man said gently. 'You are more than welcome to stay here. Travel in the morning when it is light. You yourself do not look well enough to travel further tonight and the young lady is—'

Over her head, Flavius shook his head and vaguely, as she fought to control her sobs, she heard him say, 'Thank you, but her family believe she is dead and I left them this morning without a word. I must take her home as soon as possible.'

'Of course you must,' the man's wife said as she came forward and touched Thea's arm. 'Put your gown on, my dear. And you, sir, please at least sit down and allow me to dress your arm.'

Thea pulled herself away from him with difficulty and swallowed down a sob, looking up at him through the blur of her tears. 'Oh, your face...' She put her hands up to his bruised face and then looked down at his bloody arm. 'I was—so afraid you were—dead under that chariot,' she managed to say between sobs.

'Never mind that now,' he said quietly. 'Hurry and get dressed.'

'Oh . . . yes,' she said and struggled into the tattered gown and then sat, silent but for the occasional suppressed sob, while his arm was bound up again. Somehow it seemed important that she keep her tears in check, and since that took a great effort she closed her mind to everything else.

Flavius accepted gratefully when the old man offered his cart for their use and when his arm was dressed again, he stood up with some difficulty and thanked them for their assistance and their care of Thea. 'I have nothing now to pay you for your kindness,' he said, 'but when someone returns your cart in the morning—'

'It is not necessary, sir,' he said quickly. 'It has given us great pleasure to help the young lady. I am only sorry we did not send word that she was safe, but there was no-one to send and I intended to take her home tomorrow—'

Flavius waved him silent. 'It is not important now. Thea—' He held out his hand to her and she got up and walked unsteadily into the welcoming curve of his arm. The woman gave them a blanket and Thea added her thanks in rather a daze. Outside, Flavius collected his horse and tied it to the back of the cart, and then helped her up with his good hand. The fleeting expression of pain across his face as he pulled himself up beside her, did not escape her.

'Are you all right?' she asked, as they moved off towards Rome in the deepening darkness.

He looked at her and gave a rueful smile as he put his arm around her and drew her close. 'Yes. Are you? Did they hurt you?'

Tears sprang into her eyes again. She shook her head.

'Not really,' she said shakily. 'I mean—they did not—do anything to me except—except hit me and . . .' The tears spilled over and she leaned against him and gave in to the overwhelming relief. He let her weep, knowing it was the release she needed.

'I was so afraid,' she blurted out after a little while. There were so many questions to ask, so many things to say, and she did not know how or where to begin.

He kissed the top of her head. 'It's over, Thea. Try not to think about it any more now. It is enough, for now, that you are safe. If we are to get to Rome tonight in safety I think we had better save all the questions and explanations. I am afraid I do not feel equal to keeping us on the road *and* relating the story. It is not a pretty tale, and it will keep.'

She nodded silently, and put her head on his shoulder, content that she was safe at last and in arms she could trust to protect her.

The fuss which greeted them when they arrived home in the dead of night, escorted by the group of 'vigiles' who had challenged them, completely overwhelmed her and she almost fainted into the arms of her father. Given little chance to speak or protest, she was borne away from Flavius, and despatched, with servants attending, to her room.

The next hour went by in a blur. Pontius had sent for a physician, and having established that she was not about to collapse, allowed the servants to carry her off for a soothing, if brief, session in the baths, declaring, as Flavius had, that explanations could wait.

She had emerged from the baths, her hair washed and dried and combed to a shining halo, feeling almost human once more. The physician arrived and examined her, and, satisfied that nothing more serious had happened to her beyond the blows to her head, a few cuts and bruises and a nasty fright, he applied salves, prescribed plenty of rest and told her that she was a very lucky young woman. Then he went off to see Flavius, who, he said, had seemed in a far worse state.

When he had gone, Marcus and her father came to sit with her, the latter scarcely able to speak through the emotion welling up in him and wetting his eyes.

'Flavius has told us how he found you,' Marcus began, 'And—'

'But he did not tell *me*,' she protested. 'I think I know most of what happened, but . . .'

The story was told, Thea telling her side of it and then listening in horrified silence as Marcus told her briefly, and without elaboration, of Octavia's confession of jealousy and the lengths to which she had gone to devise ways to rid herself of her sister's presence, and the final plot to send her to a horrible fate at the mercy of a greedy and unscrupulous sailor bound for Egypt.

She was shocked that her sister was capable of such vicious malice, that she could deliberately plan so unspeakable a fate for her. It was hideous. 'I don't suppose she actually planned that you would be killed,' Marcus said, 'but even she must have realised that it was likely. And that was only slightly worse than what she *did* intend to happen. She was quite convinced Flavius would marry her if you were out of the way.' He paused, and looked at her sideways, a mischievous gleam in his eyes. 'She was right to be jealous, of course,' he went on, 'If you had seen Flavius's face when he knew what she had done—and to go searching for you the way he did, in the state he is in—well, it is obvious he is in love with you!'

Thea felt herself blushing furiously, and Pontius

MY DAUGHTER THELIA

beamed happily and nodded in satisfaction. 'But how *did* he find me?' she demanded, anxious to veer the conversation away from the topic of love.

Marcus told her what Flavius had told them, Pontius putting in a detail here and there, and when he had finished she sat upright in bed and said, 'Is he still here? I want to see him.'

'In the morning,' Pontius said firmly, getting to his feet. 'He is exhausted and needs to rest. He is in Marcus's room, sleeping I trust. And you,' he patted her hand and bent to kiss her forehead, 'also must sleep. There will be plenty of time in the morning to talk of other things.'

As he and Marcus went to the door, she said suddenly: 'What—has happened to Octavia?'

'The Emperor has been lenient,' Marcus said, glancing at his father and speaking carefully, 'and agreed that she may be banished to the country, to aunt Lucilla's old place, with one of the Palace guards to make sure she stays there. It is a dreadfully remote place. She is at the Palace now and leaves tomorrow.'

'We must send word to Nero that you are safe and well,' Pontius said, and a shadow passed fleetingly across his face. 'Alas, it will not help Octavia—' Thea realised then that the past few days had cost her father dearly. Despite his obvious pleasure at seeing her safe and unharmed, he seemed to have shrunk and grown considerably older, and an ashen greyness had settled over his lined face. 'Well, you must rest,' he said, turning to the door. 'You look very tired and the past few days have been a terrible ordeal for you. Sleep now.'

But, left alone, sleep was impossible. Her mind was racing with all she had been told. Octavia's insane actions left her cold with horror. When she thought of what could have happened to her . . . She did not dwell on it, but turned her thoughts to Flavius and allowed the warmth of her love for him to dispel the chill that had settled on her. Did he really love her too? It certainly seemed like it, and she wanted so much to believe it. She went over all he had said to her that evening, in the old couple's house and on the way home—little enough really, and she found she could not remember clearly. Marcus obviously believed it, but what did he know of it? And her father—well, he would believe it because he wanted it like that.

She wondered how badly hurt he really was. Far worse than he showed, or admitted, knowing him. She lay there in the candlelight for a little while, as the house fell silent, thinking of him lying in Marcus's room and wondering if he was asleep. Delicious shivers ran over her, until suddenly she could not bear it any longer. She had to see him.

She got up and went softly to the door, opening it gingerly and stepping out into the corridor, the mosaic floor cold on her bare feet. It was dark and quiet, and she paused outside the door of Marcus's room, her heart thumping painfully. There was a faint light showing beneath it. Barely hesitating, she tapped quietly and at the brief response from within, she went in.

He was lying stretched out on the bed, nearly naked except for a towel wrapped around his waist that covered him to just above his knees. He turned his head and looked at her, and only a faint surprise showed in his battered face. Both arms were bound from elbow to wrist, there was a messy raw patch on one leg below the towel, a bandage on the other above his ankle. His ribs and chest were covered with the dark shadows of bruises and there seemed to be cuts and bruises everywhere.

'You look terrible,' she said.

He raised an eyebrow at her. 'Thank you.' He unlinked his hands and pulled himself up, an involuntary expression of pain passing across his face as he put a hand to his ribs and swung his legs round so that he sat on the edge of the bed facing her. He sighed and looked up at her with a wry half-smile. 'I am getting too old for chariot races.'

'Oh, but he deliberately—'

He shook his head and made a dismissive gesture. 'It was an accident. I was too slow. It's not important.' He looked at her and the beginnings of a smile flicked at the corner of his mouth. 'Couldn't you sleep either?'

'I—came to thank you for helping Gregor,' she said quickly, suddenly trembling. She knew exactly why she had come and it had nothing to do with Gregor.

'Did you?' His eyes narrowed slightly and he gave her a long, quizzical look. Then he said: 'I soon regretted it, you know.'

'Why?' She stared at him, startled.

'Because somewhere along the road to Ostia it occurred to me that if you had gone willingly with him it would have been my gold that enabled it to happen. It seemed a cruel irony.'

She was silent for a moment. Then, timidly, 'Did you—tell Father that it would be impossible for us to marry?' she asked, almost certain that he had not.

'No. I came here to do so the morning after you disappeared.'

'Oh!' She looked quickly away, shock draining the colour from her face. She turned away, reaching for the door handle.

'Thea.' His voice was gentle but firm and she turned slowly round and raised her eyes to his. 'That was when I believed you were in love with him. And that you hated and distrusted me. But you don't, do you?' It was not really a question.

Her throat felt dry. She swallowed and shook her head. 'No.'

'And it was not merely because I was a familiar face that you threw yourself at me this evening when I rescued you from the clutches of those unscrupulous people.'

'I was already rescued,' she pointed out with a smile, knowing that he was laughing at her. 'And they were good, kind people—'

'Look, you ungrateful young savage,' he chided, trying to keep his features in order, 'I spent all day chasing around the country looking for you, in great pain and at vast cost, and I do not want to be told that it was all for nothing!'

She giggled and shook her head. 'It was not for nothing. At least now,' she added mischievously, 'I shall not be angry when you call me savage.'

'Oh, but you are so beautiful when you are in a temper!'

'I cannot always be in a temper merely to please you!'

'Don't you wish always to please me?'

She was suddenly serious. 'Yes.' Then, avoiding his eyes and with a little half-smile, 'I thought you loved Octavia—'

'Octavia?' The mixture of amazement and incredulity in his voice made her look up at him quickly. Surely it was not so ludicrous. After all, she had seen them together often enough. In a few swift, limping strides he crossed the room and pulled her into his arms. 'You are even more of a young fool than I thought if you believe—

Why, the only times I even *spoke* to her alone I was trying to force her to stop helping you meet the gladiator!' He broke off and gave her a little shake. 'Ye gods, Thea, don't you know what you have been doing to me all these months? I cannot stand any more. The Briton has gone, Octavia is out of the way and her evil jealousy with her, and though I will doubtless live to regret it, I love you! Don't you know that yet?'

'Yes, I—' she began, but he did not let her finish. He pulled her against him and buried his face in her hair. 'All these months I have loved you and scarce realised it—thinking you hated me, blaming myself for your unhappiness here, believing you were in love with the gladiator, and not knowing—until I believed it too late—that I could not live without you.'

She was a little afraid of the thoughts that were running through her mind, of the strength of the emotions that had suddenly rushed up inside her. 'I love you,' she muttered against his chest, half-afraid of the words and every muscle in her body tense. 'I have loved you for weeks and known it very well. But I thought—I believed it was Octavia you loved. And she said you were only amusing yourself with me and only wished to—to get me into your bed. And so it seemed from the way you treated me when you were not kissing me—like a child. You seemed to think I could never be anything other than a Iceni "savage"—'

He pushed her away from him and tilted her head until she looked up at him, and he cupped her face in his hands. 'Certainly I wish to take you to my bed,' he said softly, 'and I would not have you any other way than an unruly young savage!'

'I was so afraid,' she said, 'So afraid that you were dead when that chariot . . .'

He smiled, and his hungry gaze moved over her face, taking in every detail. 'I do not die so easily,' he replied, 'otherwise I am afraid you would have murdered me in the woods that day!'

How long ago it seemed! Tentatively she put up a hand to the little scar. 'It has healed well.'

He bent his head to kiss her, gently at first but almost immediately growing hungry and demanding and she responded eagerly, until he groaned and drew away, setting her from him. 'Thea, Thea . . . I told you before I am a mere mortal. I do not have so much control. We can be wed tomorrow—'

'Yes,' she sighed, a little breathless.

'Sweet Venus, do not look like that! I am supposed to stay here tonight and I do not think I can sleep knowing you are but a few paces away—'

'If—if we are to be wed tomorrow,' she began softly, and then stopped, blushing, and lowered her eyes in confusion, wondering at herself that she could have such a thought.

He threw back his head and laughed, and caught her up into his arms again, only to release her abruptly, wincing. 'You had better be gentle with me, then,' he said with a wry smile, 'for I have bruises in the most accursed places!'

A mischievous light gleamed in her eyes. 'But I thought you were a Roman!' she cried. 'Romans are strong and fearless and invincible. They rape every woman they see and eat babies for breakfast! Yet here is one who whimpers at a few trifling little scratches and begs a mere weakling girl to be gentle with him!' She dodged away from him easily, giggling; and then squealed as he caught her wrist and pulled her roughly towards him. 'Oh, you are very daring while I am in such a state!' he exclaimed, half warning half promising. 'Are our children going to be as impossibly wicked as you?'

'I hope not!' she declared in horror. 'I am afraid they would be a great deal of trouble!'

'Never mind. I intend to make you the mother of a whole brood of unmanageable brats!' He kissed her again, crushing her against his chest, heedless this time of the pain, and his mouth bruising hers, searching, demanding, probing. His hands moved caressingly over her tingling body, seeking the fullness of her breasts that seemed to ache for his touch; and a glowing warmth stole through her as she gave herself up to the sensual pleasure that made her skin burn deliciously through the shift.

He drew her towards the bed, shedding the towel and awkwardly trying to remove her shift with one hand, reluctant to free her mouth from his hungry kiss.

'Let me,' she offered, and pulled away, shedding the offending garment quickly. 'I do not know how we are to go about it if you cannot even—' She broke off with a scream as he caught her arm and threw her onto the bed.

'Be quiet, idiot!' he hissed as he extinguished the candle. 'Do you want your father to catch us?'

For answer, she pulled him down to her, and his laughing protests and winces of pain made her giggle and she quickly lost any lingering nervousness she may have had amongst a tangle of limbs and covers, abandoning herself to the will of the man who, tomorrow, she would call husband.

Masquerade Historical Romances

New romances from bygone days

Masquerade Historical Romances, published by Mills & Boon, vividly recreate the romance of our past. These are the two superb new stories to look out for next month.

THE VALLEY OF TEARS
Valentina Luellen
SPY FOR CROMWELL
Caroline Martin

Buy them from your usual paperback stockist, or write to: Mills & Boon Reader Service, P.O. Box 236, Thornton Rd, Croydon, Surrey CR9 3RU, England. Readers in South Africa-write to: Mills & Boon Reader Service of Southern Africa, Private Bag X3010, Randburg, 2125.

Mills & Boon
the rose of romance